MIDNIGHT QUEST

LISA MARIE RICE

Midnight Quest ©2016 by Lisa Marie Rice (Second Edition).

Published by Lisa Marie Rice

Cover Design & Formatting
by Sweet 'N Spicy Designs

To my son David, the filmmaker. Live long and prosper, my darling.

CHAPTER ONE

Portland, Oregon

It was a surprise, coming home early. She wasn't expecting him until tomorrow night. Morton "Jacko" Jackman closed the front door behind him and quietly walked into the house to look for Lauren, the woman who held his heart.

It had been a long week. A Monday-to-Friday job advising a bank in Tijuana on security. He was supposed to fly back on Friday evening, tomorrow. But Jacko had missed Lauren ferociously and had worked eighteen-hour days in order to wrap things up and get away at noon today. He'd made his way back home by flying south to Guadalajara and then back north to Portland via Los Angeles. It had been a three-flight, nine-hour slog instead of a three-hour direct flight, just to spend an extra night at home.

But man, was it worth it. Worth every second of transiting through dismal, crowded airports and sitting in cramped airline seats eating cheap, crap cookies and drinking weak, lukewarm sludge. All forgotten in an instant because…there she was.

Just look at her, he thought, sitting in her pretty little study, working at her computer.

She didn't know he was there. Jacko was naturally quiet—he was a trained sniper, after all—and she hadn't heard him come in. He watched her working, silently absorbed.

He just loved looking at her when she was focused on a drawing or watercolor. She looked like she was channeling some higher power. Like magic was beaming down to earth through her.

She was listening to music, a Bach concerto. Now wasn't that a kick in the ass, him recognizing Bach? Before Lauren, Limp Bizkit was more his style. The only classics he knew were AC/DC and Guns N' Roses. But now he could tell Bach from Mozart from Beethoven. Bach, Mozart, Beethoven. Dead white guys, all of them, but now part of his life.

Lauren was drawing on a tablet, the results showing on the monitor. She was designing a book cover. It was a sideline that was really taking off and she had a list of clients as long as his dick. She sometimes consulted him, though the fuck he knew about book covers? Whatever he managed to mumble in response, she always thanked him and went back to work, saying he'd helped her define what she wanted.

They Skyped every evening he was in Tijuana and last night she said she'd gotten the commission to design covers for a fantasy trilogy, *The Ironlands*.

What she had so far was striking. A dusky-skinned woman with a strong face, dark hair around her shoulders, one silver streak of hair across her forehead, matching silver eyes. Beautiful, resolute, those amazing eyes seemed to watch him from across the room. *The Iron Princess* was the title, in what seemed letters cast in iron. She looked exactly like someone who could rule over The Ironlands.

Jacko cocked his head to see better but his movement must have created some kind of disturbance in the force, because Lauren suddenly lifted her head and turned around.

And her face lit up with joy. Just...*lit up*. Like Jacko had brought Christmas and her birthday and the Fourth of July with him. Pure joy.

No one ever lit up at the sight of him. In the Teams, the guys were happy to see him, sure, because when he turned up, it meant that the tango a thousand yards out was going to get whacked. Other than that, his colleagues at ASI were fine with working with him, having a beer and playing poker with him. But their faces didn't light up when they saw him. Only Lauren's did that.

He rubbed his chest for a second, because something hurt inside, then braced himself as Lauren stood up and ran to him. Two steps away, she threw herself at him, knowing he'd catch her.

Oh yeah, he'd catch her. Always.

As his arms closed around her, that low-level anxiety he felt when he was away from her dissipated like smoke in the wind. Jacko didn't do anxiety, except when it came to Lauren. The possibility of something bad happening to her, of losing her, was the only thing he was really afraid of.

When he was out of town, he always had this crazy worry.

Though, *get real*, he told himself. When an ASI guy had to go out of town, his teammates banded together to make sure his lady was safe. Every time he talked to headquarters, they made sure he knew Lauren was okay. Isabel and Felicity had stopped by the house several times and Lauren had been to dinner at Isabel and Joe's. He'd gotten a mouthwatering description of the menu, too. And he Skyped Lauren every evening. So, yeah, he knew she'd been safe.

But he missed her all the same. Ferociously.

Lauren was laughing as he twirled her around, soft dark hair belling. "You're early! Oh my gosh, I wasn't expecting you until tomorrow night. How'd you get away so quickly? Did you have to shoot someone?"

"Nope." He smiled down into her silver-blue eyes. "I was a good boy. Didn't shoot anyone, promise. I just got everything done I had to do and came home early, that's all."

"But surely your trip—"

He kissed her. She was going to fuss over whether his trip had been inconvenient and tedious and tiring, and yes, it had been all of that. He didn't want to talk about it and kissing her was the best possible distraction. Throw her off course.

The kiss distracted him, too.

God.

When his mouth touched hers, he got that mild electric shock he always got when he touched her. Like she was the conduit for some otherworldly source of energy, and maybe she was, because his life felt flat when she wasn't there.

He kissed her until he felt he was melting into her, until she turned boneless in his arms

He was learning about this couple thing. Though he had a hard-on you could hammer nails with, he didn't walk into the bedroom with her in his arms, strip her and fall on top of her.

Nope, he'd learned better. Though the sense of urgency was still there, he knew she wasn't going anywhere, which was a turn-on in itself. At the beginning of their relationship, Jacko took her to bed every single time he could, as fast as he could. It seemed impossible to him that a woman as beautiful and smart as Lauren would stick around.

One of these days she would ask herself what she was doing with a roughneck like him and she'd dump him. So he was going to get as much sex in as possible, before she cut him off.

But...Lauren had stayed. Lauren was with him, forever if he had anything to say about it. So mostly he tried to hold off a little on throwing her on the bed and jumping on top of her as soon as he saw her, which was more or less what he'd done constantly in the beginning. Not cool.

Now he felt he could show a little restraint because, well, she wasn't going anywhere.

He tasted his welcome in her mouth, soft and sweet. She was happy to see him. The long, tedious trip was worthwhile because he'd gained twenty-four hours with Lauren he wouldn't have otherwise had.

His arms started tightening around her when she pulled away. Rose in her cheeks, laughter in her eyes. "I think I know why you came home early."

He smiled down at her. "Yeah, that too. But I was done and I just wanted to come home fast as I could."

Home. This was the first home he'd ever had. He'd never told her that, but his Lauren was smart. She knew. "Wanted to see how you were doing with that cover you said you were working on. From what I could see before you threw yourself at me, it's looking pretty good."

She swatted him on the arm. "I didn't *throw* myself at you, I was just happy to see you."

"Did too throw yourself at me," he answered smugly and smiled when she rolled her eyes. "So show me what you've done so far."

Lauren turned and went to her workstation. She had three computer screens on a pretty oak table up against a corkboard on the wall. The corkboard was filled with sketches and watercolors. Jacko knew her work method by now and could follow her idea as clearly as if she'd explained it. He could see the first sketches, quick pencil drafts, a featureless face in left profile, right profile and full frontal. She took the full frontal and sketched various expressions and features. At the bottom was a detailed drawing of an attractive woman, unsmiling, with strong features.

Then she went to her graphics tablet and the end result was on the central monitor. The finished cover, striking and unique. He had no difficulty imagining the woman as the Iron Princess of a faraway land of magic and dragons. A woman made to rule, a woman of destiny.

It was amazing. Lauren took pencils and watercolors and computer pixels and created magic.

Jacko kept one arm around Lauren and reached out with his other hand to touch the monitor.

"This is gorgeous, honey. Very powerful. The writer will love it."

"You think so?" Lauren's head was cocked as she studied the image, leaning against him. But she was flushed with pleasure as she looked up at him. "I was going to ask you a favor. Was going to bribe you with food. Isabel brought over some five-grain bread and some gorgonzola mousse."

Jacko shook his head. "You don't need to bribe me." God no. He'd do anything for her. All she had to do was ask. "What do you need?"

He'd welcome the chance to do something for her. So far it was really lopsided. She'd given him a beautiful home, took care of him better than he deserved, loved him. That was the biggie. He loved her too, but damn—look at her. She was really easy to love. And he wasn't. When he and Lauren went out, they got plenty of looks. Some discreet, some not. And in every single head, he could read the thought—*what's a girl like her doing with a guy like that?*

"Well, the book is set on an Earth-like planet where there is one huge island. And she wants a hand-drawn map of the island, like old-timey treasure maps. I could do it but you're really good at drawing maps. I've read the book and I know the geography so we could work on it together." She frowned up at him. "So do you think you could hand-draw a map for me?"

He'd rip out his lungs for her. Kill for her. Die for her. This? No biggie.

"Sure, honey. It'd be fun." Would, too.

"Cool! We can start on that over the weekend."

"Maybe even tomorrow. I reported in that I got the job done early and would be in tomorrow and Senior said just the morning. Afternoon is covered."

"Wow. A whole afternoon off. You okay with that?" Lauren knew—everyone knew—that he loved his job. Taking time off was not a thing Jacko did.

"Yep. I can do some stuff around the house. The Beast needs a tune-up and I wanted to install that new sound system in the rec room." An extra afternoon off—that would have pinged his pain-o-meter a couple of years ago. Now it was just some extra time to do his thing.

Lauren smiled up at him. "I do hope you realize that a free Friday afternoon will inevitably be followed by a free Saturday and Sunday. You won't freak, will you?"

Jacko had a sudden vision of keeping Lauren in bed for forty-eight hours straight. Eating in bed, having sex, showering, repeat. For two days. Feasting on Lauren like she was a chocolate treat, hours and hours and hours of sex.

It made him slightly dizzy. That was exactly how they were going to spend the weekend—in bed.

"I'll cope. I'll think of something." She narrowed her eyes at the sudden thickness of his voice. It was naturally deep—Lauren called him a human woofer—and the blood that left his head to go straight to his dick made his voice rasp. She was visibly trying not to look at his groin. Her cheeks colored a deep pink.

Her pretty mouth opened but nothing came out.

Shit.

She enjoyed their sex life. Jacko made sure of it. But she wasn't up for sex every single second of every single day the way he was. Not home five minutes and he was petitioning not very subtly for an immediate lay. The fuck was wrong with him?

"Hey." He made his voice smooth. "Anything to eat? I'm starving."

"Oh!" Lauren immediately lost that slightly stunned look and snapped into motion. "Of course! I didn't know you were coming this evening but I made some really good vegetable soup and like I said, Isabel gave me a loaf of her five-grain bread." She reached up to kiss his cheek then dropped back down to her pretty bare feet. "Why don't you take a shower and everything will be ready when you come out?"

He kissed her forehead and headed toward the bathroom, feeling like a real shit. It had been so easy to distract her. All he ever had to do was hint at the fact that he was hungry or thirsty or needed anything at all and she immediately hustled to surround him with creature comforts. She took pride in making him happy, not knowing that just her breathing was enough to make him happy.

This couple thing was hard. No wonder he'd never tried it before. It was particularly hard when he lost control when he was around Lauren. Just a little. But just a little was a lot for Jacko. He'd forged his own life, step by painful step, every single second of the way exercising iron control.

He'd been brought up in a broken-down trailer park in a dusty shithole in Texas. Everything— every single thing—he had in life, he'd carved out of the face of the rock with his bare hands. He hadn't even been brought up, in the sense most people had. His druggie mother drifted in and out of his life, and he'd had to see to his own upbringing. He'd been a troublemaker, barreling straight toward juvie when Sheriff Pendleton had said, "Son, it's either the military or jail. Choose now."

So Jacko had joined the Navy and finally found his place.

Losing control around Lauren was not allowed. She was the best thing that had ever happened to him—even better than making it into the SEALs— and he was not going to fuck this up.

Lauren went into the kitchen and he walked into the bedroom. *Their* bedroom, though you couldn't really tell he lived here. Pure chickville.

Flowers in vases, silver bowls with dried flower petals, pretty, delicate furniture. A chair that Lauren called a nursing chair for some reason, which he was terrified to sit on. A big bed with flowered sheets.

If someone had told him a year ago that he'd sleep between flowered sheets, he'd have punched his lights out. But here he was, sleeping between flowered sheets, and there were flounces around the bed. He'd never even seen them before. Didn't even know they were called that.

The Navy was not a place for flounces around beds. A cot in the barracks with a trunk at the foot of the cot. That was his sleeping quarters in the military. And once he got out and started working for ASI, his own bachelor pad had been super spare with a couch, high-end TV and big plain bed with black sheets.

But living in a real girly place didn't bug him as much as he thought it would. He worked in a high-testosterone business, so a touch of chick vibe was fine. More than fine, actually, because it was like being with Lauren even when she wasn't there, like now.

He unpacked and put things away fast. Good thing the Navy had pounded neatness into him. The trailer he'd grown up in had looked like weasels nested there. It had taken him all of a week—and 250 pushups, because he hadn't known how to stow stuff and had to learn fast through pain, the Navy way—to understand and practice neatness. It was a habit by now.

The bathroom was another testosterone-free place. Lauren had more lotions and creams and makeup gear than he had weapons, and that was saying something. It smelled really nice, too.

Showers in the 'Stan had been gross. Smelling of toe fungus and jism because everyone jerked off in the showers. Which was always better than jerking off into the sheets. They got hard and stiff. One of Jacko's teammates had had sheets so stiff they crumbled and broke.

Lauren had stopped that cold. Now that he had her, he couldn't give himself a hand job. Just couldn't. It felt like cheating, even if he was only cheating on her with a big calloused hand, not another woman.

So he stood under the shower and lathered himself with one of her flower-scented soaps that smelled like her, looking down occasionally at his hard-on and sighing. Showers were quick and there was no need to dry his hair since he shaved his head.

Five minutes after stepping under the water, having willed the hard-on down by thinking of the 'Stan, and he was in clean sweats, walking into the kitchen.

Man, everything in this house smelled great.

The dining room table was decorated with a pink tablecloth and a small vase of flowers. There was a wooden cheese platter and an omelet she'd whipped up fast. She was ladling soup into their bowls and it smelled like heaven.

Lauren looked up with a smile as he walked into the room. "I hope you're as hungry as you said. There's about a gallon of soup. And it's a six-egg omelet."

Jacko took in everything at a glance. His beautiful woman, watching his eyes, the pretty table, the food he knew for a fact was going to be delicious.

"I thought you were coming home tomorrow," she said with a slight smile. She was watching his face carefully. "I was planning a special dinner for you."

He bent down, kissed her. "I can't imagine anything more special than this," he said truthfully. "Everything looks great." A thought suddenly occurred to him and he looked at her just as carefully. "Was the special dinner supposed to be for a special occasion?"

His heart started pounding hard and heavy in his chest. He could feel his fingertips tingle.

He'd asked her to marry him many times. It had become a joke. They shared everything—a bed, a home, a life. She'd even said yes…*but.* Yes, but not right now. Yes, but it was a big step. Yes, but things were just fine the way they were.

She was going to say "yes" without a "but". He could feel it. She had a glow to her, as if something special had been switched on inside.

Jacko had no idea where this obsession with marriage came from. He'd never been a marrying kind of guy. SEAL marriages were rare and usually didn't last long. One of his teammates had been divorced four times.

Jacko had been in his thirties and employed at ASI before he'd even seen a happy marriage. Two of them, in fact. ASI's bosses—John Huntington, aka "Midnight Man", and Douglas Kowalski, aka "the Senior"—were both very happily married. The few married couples Jacko had seen growing up back in Cross, Texas had been shit unhappy. Most marriages there'd been toxic, some so dysfunctional the bad vibes were almost visible. The marriages he'd seen had been fueled by lust, alcohol and rage, the same things breaking the couple apart.

His own mom hadn't married. She'd been toxic enough for two people, though.

Marriage hadn't even been a blip on his horizon until Lauren. And now look at him. He was worse than a girl pining for a husband. He pined for a wife. Lauren. It pained him when he introduced her as his girlfriend, because she wasn't. She was more than that. He'd had plenty of girlfriends— well...mostly fuck buddies, but still—and they were light-years from what Lauren was to him.

He wanted to call her his wife. He wanted everyone in the world to know that she was his and would be until the end of time. He wanted other men to look at her and understand that *Back off motherfucker, she's taken* was written in invisible letters on her forehead.

He knew it made him an asshole, but it didn't change his feelings at all.

He'd asked Lauren to marry him and she was finally going to accept.

Hot damn.

Yeah, they were going to celebrate that tomorrow night, in the best way possible. In bed. For hours.

Blood shot back to his dick, so sudden it almost made him feel dizzy. Massive transfer of blood from big head to little head.

She smiled at him, one of those mysterious smiles only she ever managed to produce. "Sort of a special occasion, yes. You'll be happy."

Fuck yeah, he'd be happy.

Well, he'd sort of taken a vow not to jump on her like a wolverine, but he needed something to calm down his hormones. He'd eat his way out of this.

He pulled out Lauren's chair then sat down and powered his way through the meal. Lauren asked him about the business trip and he told her what he could. The security measures he'd installed were top of the line and top secret, too. They were worthy of a US Embassy. But she didn't want to know the technical details of bank security. She wanted to know if he'd gotten along with the bank president and the bank employees. He had, to his surprise. He hadn't punched anyone, not once. His social skills were coming right along, another thing to thank Lauren for.

"So I guess the bank president is going to be grateful to you, if they've been robbed nine times in the past year."

Jacko broke off a chunk of the bread to accompany the omelet. "If they get robbed again, I'll eat my hat. And if they're stiffed by one of their own employees, they'll know who." He popped the bread in his mouth.

"Wow, I guess they didn't feed you down Mexico way, did they?" Lauren teased as she started pulling stuff out of the fridge.

"They fed me," Jacko protested, looking with interest at what she was setting on the table.

"Clearly not enough."

In the end, he demolished half a Camembert, another half loaf of Isabel's five-grain bread, a big bowl of tomato salad, half the omelet and a square of frozen eggplant parmesan Lauren nuked in the microwave.

Lauren sat back, watched him and shook her head when he finished. "Guess you're still a growing boy."

"I'm grown," he growled. Oh yeah. He was 240 pounds of pure muscle, and right now he felt very grown up. He could feel every single male hormone in his body.

Okay. It was time. He'd been a good boy. He'd waited, they'd had a nice meal together—though Lauren had stopped eating half an hour ago—but now it was time.

He stood, aware that his groin was at eye level and that his erection was very visible in his sweats. Lauren's eyes widened as she looked at his crotch and his dick gave a kick in his pants. Her gaze moved up to meet his and as she saw his face, she blushed a fiery red.

Jacko didn't know many women who could blush, and was surprised that Lauren still could, considering how often they had sex together.

He got it that she hadn't had that active a sex life before him. She often said that she felt like he'd found her "on" switch. But it also meant that he tried to be careful with her. If she was blushing, that meant he should go slow.

Jacko was raring to go after five days of abstinence, but Lauren didn't work like that. She needed to get used to him all over again. It had to be one of those go-slow times.

Jacko held out his hands and her eyebrows went up as she put her hands in his. She thought he'd carry her to bed, which he sometimes did. It was his way to get them into the bedroom as fast as possible, though he knew she thought it was romantic.

Not romantic. Practical.

But Jacko could do romance.

He brought her hand to his mouth, watching her eyes as he kissed it. She smiled at him. Oh yeah. He bent to kiss her, just the lightest touch of her lips, and she sighed and closed her eyes. Jacko put his mouth to her ear, kissed it, then whispered, "Come to bed with me?"

She shivered and sighed. "Oh yes, darling."

If Jacko had followed his own desires, they'd already be on the bed having sex. But this was nice, too. Hearing her sigh, having her smile at him. Yeah.

He left a bedside lamp on in the bedroom. He loved looking at her, watching how her body changed for him.

He tunneled his hands in her hair, holding her head for his kiss. "I missed you so much," he said when he lifted his head.

Lauren laughed and pressed her hips against his. "Yeah. I can tell."

"What about you, hmm?" She could feel his massive hard-on. When chicks were turned on, it was harder to tell. "Did you miss me?"

Jacko was suddenly dying to read her body. It was like a book, only better. Her body told him everything he needed to know.

He unzipped her sweat suit top, pulling the zipper down slowly, watching her eyes. She huffed out a little breath when the top opened. But Jacko huffed like a bull when he saw she wasn't wearing a bra. God. He opened the top, sliding it off her shoulders, and tried to keep his breathing under control. Keeping everything under control—his breathing, his hands, his dick—seemed nearly impossible in moments like these. Like patting his head and rubbing his stomach.

She was just so goddamn beautiful, all that pale, smooth skin, plump breasts, hard little nipples. He rubbed his thumb over the nipples, enjoying feeling her shudder. They were hard as little rocks. "Yeah," he said, trying to keep the smugness out of his voice, "you missed me."

Her eyes were half closed. "You touch me a little further down and you'll see exactly how much I missed you."

Jacko closed his own eyes. She sometimes blindsided him like that. "Yeah," he whispered. He ran his hands down her sides, taking the sweatpants and pretty lace panties down her long legs. She stepped out of them and there she was, naked and welcoming.

"Feel me, Jacko." Lauren shifted so her legs were apart. "Feel how much I want you."

He ran his hand over her belly and slid it over her mound, feeling the soft ash-colored hairs. Lauren was a natural blonde and her sex was covered in a trim little cloud of light-colored hair. She'd dyed her hair dark before coming to Portland in an effort to disguise herself. She'd been on the run from a psychopath and had done everything in her power to change her look.

She'd asked him lots of times if he wanted her to go back to being a blonde but he liked her exactly the way she was when he'd first met her. That Snow White look—pale skin, dark hair, silver-blue eyes—turned him on so much he didn't ever want her to change. And that contrast between her dark hair and that light cloud only he knew about—that was his own delicious secret.

He gave her a tiny push on the shoulder and she understood, settling back on the bed, spread out for him like a feast.

"Clothes."

They understood each other perfectly. In a second he was naked, too, dick a thick column jutting out from his belly. Her eyes traveled slowly from his face down his body, and her smile grew when her gaze reached his dick and it gave a kick as new blood rushed down to it.

Lauren laughed.

Jacko reached down with his hand and placed it on her thigh, right next to her sex and she sighed.

He took a moment to study her, this woman who'd completely upended his life. She was so much more beautiful now that she'd put on a little weight. That first night he'd been almost frightened at how fragile she looked naked. Being on the run from a psychopath would do that. He could count her ribs. Lying flat like this, her hipbones had jutted out and her belly had been a hollow. Her bones had felt like bird bones.

Now she was an ivory-skinned goddess.

What did you do with a goddess? Worship her.

He fell to his knees and pulled her legs toward him until they bracketed his chest, her sex right at the edge of the bed like a tempting pearl.

She was glistening, all pink and wet. He traced the rim of her sex with his finger and watched, fascinated, as more moisture welled up and the folds turned deep pink. As he touched her, her head pressed back against the mattress and that long slender neck arched back.

He circled her again. "Did you touch yourself while I was gone?" he asked hoarsely. Because he couldn't fuck his hand, but maybe she could touch herself. It was all a pale imitation of what they could do when they were together, but it was something.

"No." She shook her head. There was a slight rasp as her hair slid across the pillow case. "I couldn't. I was waiting for you."

"Yeah," he said. "It's not the same."

"Not even close."

He put his hands on the inside of her thighs. They were dark and rough against her pale soft skin, an erotic contrast. His hands framed her sex, open to him. A temptation he couldn't resist.

He kissed her there, exactly like he kissed her mouth, tongue deep inside her. He made a noise against her skin, a hungry noise, and he felt her muscles contract against his mouth. This time she made the noise.

"Jacko!" Her hands grabbed his head.

He breathed deeply, taking in her scent. When she was aroused, she smelled like no other woman he'd ever known—sweet and salty and a little like the ocean. He moved even closer, kissing her more deeply, and she clenched around him again. Her thighs started trembling against the palms of his hands and he pulled away, just a little. God, there was nothing more gorgeous. She was wet with her own juices and his mouth, shiny and pink. He brushed his thumb against her clitoris and watched, fascinated, as her tissues closed like a fist then opened again.

She was close.

He licked her, gave her a tiny little bite that made her shake, then shifted up her body and entered her fast, kissing her mouth, feeling her climax against his dick and feeling the climax with his mouth and then he was feeling it all over, in her arms and legs clutching him, in the fast heartbeat against his chest, in the fingers curling into the muscles of his shoulder.

He settled into a driving rhythm but when she whispered, "Welcome home, my darling," it was like setting off a detonator and all he could do was hold himself tightly against her, inside her, while he exploded.

CHAPTER TWO

Jacko never, ever admitted to being tired. But Lauren could tell by the quality of his sleep if he was tired or not. After making love, he'd fallen into a sleep so deep it told her what it had cost him to work so hard and spend so many hours traveling just so he could come home to her sooner.

He loved her.

She smiled at the ceiling as the early morning light slowly filled the room.

Jacko loved her, and soon there would be another person in her life, another love. She hugged the thought to herself, happy beyond words. The kit had told her she was pregnant but she already knew that. Her body told her, told her that she and Jacko had made a human being. A baby, to love and protect. To watch over as he or she grew up. She listened to her heart beating in her chest and wondered whether later, when the baby was fully formed inside her womb, their heartbeats would align.

Loving Jacko was already overwhelming. He filled her life, all the cracks and crevices. He made her whole and happy.

But a child? Oh God, who knew? She felt like she could touch the sky, like she'd been brushed by magic. She'd burst into tears of happiness when she saw the wand turn pink and as she touched her belly, it was like the universe coalesced under her fingertips.

Last night it had taken all her self-discipline not to tell Jacko immediately. She was bursting with the news. She'd wanted to call Isabel and Felicity and Summer right away but it wasn't fair for them to know before Jacko did.

He was going to be a father. He'd make a wonderful father, just as he'd make a wonderful husband. This was the moment to decide on the wedding as well. Why had she held back? For some reason, she simply couldn't say the words, couldn't set a date. She thought maybe it was some superstitious thing—too much happiness all at once, tempting the gods to destroy that happiness. But that wasn't it.

She'd been waiting. And now the waiting was over. She knew it was exactly the right moment for them to become a family.

She sighed in delight.

"Someone's happy this morning."

Lauren turned her head and saw Jacko shaking his head. She grinned at him. He looked a little taken aback. Did she smile so seldom? Well, that was going to change, and soon.

"Yeah. I'm happy. I'm particularly happy that you're back."

"Yeah?" The sleepiness disappeared from his voice and that deep, sexy tone he got when he thought of sex took its place. He threw back the covers. "Exactly how happy are you?"

She hadn't bothered to put pajamas on, and he looked at her naked body with pleasure.

"Why don't you find out?" When Jacko turned her on, her voice dropped an octave and she sounded like Mae West. She'd never heard that tone coming from her mouth before, but now it seemed like a permanent feature. "You being such an observant man and all."

The sound that came out of Jacko's throat sounded like a lion purring. "Oh yeah."

He placed his broad palm against her throat and slowly drew his hand down the center of her chest until it lay against her belly.

His eyes followed his hand as he spoke. "You know, last night I was thinking how much more beautiful you are now that you've put on a few pounds. That first time—you were so thin and fragile. I was afraid I'd break a bone. Now you're just so…luscious."

His hand flexed on her belly, opening and closing.

There was no way she could keep this secret a second longer. It was exploding out of her.

"Jacko," she said seriously, and placed her hand over his. Their hands made such a contrast. Hers pale and half the size of his. His eyes met hers, slightly puzzled at her tone.

"I *have* put a few pounds on and ordinarily I'd swat you for noticing." She looked down at herself then back up at him. "But what you're seeing is not a weight gain. What you're seeing is my body changing. Because, my darling, I'm pregnant. We're going to have a baby."

His hand lifted off her belly, a swift and uncontrollable gesture, like lifting a hand away from a hot surface.

Of all the reactions possible, she hadn't imagined this one. His face turned blank—utterly and completely blank. As if he'd gone somewhere else and happened to leave his face behind.

She sat up. "Jacko?"

His jaw muscles contracted, as if he were biting back words. "That's—that's great, honey." The words were the right ones, except they were coming out of that stiff, expressionless face.

"Jacko, what's the matter?" Lauren reached out to touch his shoulder but he'd already moved away. He rolled off the bed and started pulling on his jeans. "Jacko?" This time she couldn't keep the trembling out of her voice.

He was pulling on one of his long-sleeved tees then tying his boot laces.

"Gotta go in early, honey." He leaned down to give her a kiss that was over immediately. "See you tonight. I'll come home early."

And in a second he was gone.

It was a good thing Jacko was an excellent driver and that he could drive from home to the office blindfolded, because that was basically what he was doing. No cloth over his eyes, but he still didn't see anything on the road. He avoided collisions through sheer instinct.

His brain wasn't working right. He'd simply blanked out. Mind gone. That had never happened to him before, a shock so great he was taken away from himself. Ever under fire, he was in total control of himself, but right now he couldn't control anything about himself, not even his movements.

He hadn't seen the intersections, the other drivers or pedestrians. All he could see was Lauren. Pregnant with their child, having their child, dying in childbirth. The child massively deformed, a monster. A murderous monster.

The nightmare repeated itself right in front of his eyes, over and over again. Hi-def, 3D, with a soundtrack.

Rushing a screaming, bleeding Lauren to the hospital, staying by her side until the doctors kicked him out of the operating theater, waiting outside, heart hammering, crazy with terror, the tired surgeon coming out, pulling down his mask, sad eyes telling the truth before his mouth could.

Because, well, any child of his would have tainted blood. Fuck yeah—how could it not? Jacko had no idea who his father was but odds were that good old dad was a junkie, just like his mom. Some drug-crazed loser, passing through town. His mom had never been comfortable with normal people. She was too far gone, lost in the smoky hell of addiction and craziness, to ever be with normal people. There was no helping her, either.

Sheriff Pendleton had tried over and over again, getting her into the few state-sponsored rehab programs, keeping an eye out for Jacko, helping when he could. His mom baited the sheriff, spat at him, called him names.

She hadn't been choosy over who she fucked. Any dick would do as long as the guy attached to it would buy her a drink or supply her with something to get high, accompanied by a few bucks, which never went toward food.

So his father could have been anybody, and probably the furthest thing possible from a good guy.

Jacko lost count of the number of times she'd been declared an unfit mother. He'd transited in and out of foster homes until he found his final home in the Navy. She'd sober up just long enough to get him back to qualify for child support, then she'd go right back to turning tricks and getting high. And when she discovered meth, not even child support could coax her back to the world of the living.

She'd died of an overdose but by then, Jacko was long gone to the Navy, intent on becoming a SEAL.

They'd waited until he passed Hell Week and then the Senior had taken him aside and given him the news. The Senior had an idea what Jacko's mom was like and hadn't offered condolences. There were none to offer. Jacko's mom had been dead long before her body gave in to the drugs and liquor.

She'd been dead and buried two weeks by the time the news came to Jacko. It hadn't been easy to find him. He hadn't even put her down as next of kin. Doing the paperwork for enlistment, the clerk had looked at him, startled, when he read the stark form. Next of kin: none.

That was Jacko's heritage—a crazy druggie for a mom and an unknown john for a dad. Great stuff to be putting into an innocent kid's veins.

Jacko had known that sooner or later Lauren would be wanting kids. She was a normal woman and normal women wanted children. But she was on contraception shots and Jacko just…put the idea off. Straight out of his head. He'd been meaning to sound Lauren out about not having kids at all, seeing whether she could wrap her head around it. What did they need a kid for anyway? They were really happy just as they were. He was going to press that case, see if she'd buy it.

And if she didn't—well.

Yeah. He hadn't thought that one through.

Jacko was a sniper. Snipers planned. They were thorough and careful and calm. They planned for every single possibility, but man, he'd dropped the ball here. He couldn't face the thought of kids, not with his heritage, so he hadn't thought about them at all.

Denial was not a good trait for a soldier to have. Denial got you killed.

A *kid*.

Christ.

What the fuck was he going to do with a kid? If it took after Lauren, fine. Fabulous in fact. A mini version of Lauren, hell yeah. He could get behind that. But what if the kid took after him? What then? And who the fuck was he, anyway?

Lauren had very pretty long-fingered, elegant hands. She always said her hands were just like her mother's hands.

Jacko stared at his own hands on the steering wheel. They were big and dark, broad-palmed, strong. He couldn't recall his mother's hands and who the fuck knew if they were like his father's hands?

And they were trembling. His fucking hands were fucking trembling. So what was that about? His hands didn't tremble, not even in fucking *firefights*. Nope, they were steady as rocks. But now? Shaking like he had the DTs.

The rest of him was shaking too. He was shaking and sweaty and his hands were slippery on the wheel. A huge metal band around his chest made it hard to breathe. He wasn't in any condition to drive.

Jacko swerved fast to the curb and killed the engine, pressing back in his seat. He lifted his hands from the steering wheel and held them in front of his face, watching them tremble, his whole body coated in the cold sweat of stress. He'd call it the sweat of panic, except Jacko didn't do panic.

Still, it felt a lot like panic. Or what he knew of panic. He'd never felt it himself, but some guys panicked in battle or in the aftermath. He'd seen them. Sweating, trembling, eyes wide. Tunnel-visioning, incapable of responding to the environment, lost.

Like he was, right now.

His heart was hammering in his chest, thumping against his rib cage, beating harder and faster than ever before in his life. His heart rate had been measured at sixty beats per minute after an hour's training cycle with live fire.

And now? He put a finger to his pulse and counted.

Fuck. One-twenty. His heart was beating faster than after a ten-mile run. Faster than his heart had ever been measured. Like all SEALs, he'd been measured and tested and weighed and analyzed to death. Nothing in his life could make his heart race like this. Maybe a massive hemorrhage, his heart frantically pumping to make up for the blood loss. Other than that? Nothing.

Except here he was, stopped by the side of the road, heart flailing around in his chest, covered in sweat. Heart pounding.

Jacko smacked the steering wheel hard. Good thing it was sturdy because he put all his frustration behind the blow, and he was strong. He thumped it again. He felt like ripping it away from the steering column. He felt like taking out his Glock and fucking shooting it. Or shooting something. Or kicking something.

His skin was too tight and too hot. He buzzed down his windows and let in the winter air but it was still too hot. He climbed out of the vehicle and stood stock still, eyes unfocused in the cold rain until he realized he was on a major route and cars had been whizzing by for God only knew how long. A foghorn-like blast and a truck whooshed by, spraying him with icy water. He caught a glimpse of an angry face and uplifted fist. The guy was pissed and he was right.

Jacko checked his watch.

Shit. He'd been standing by the side of the road for half an hour. Like in a freaking trance.

What the fuck was *wrong* with him?

Lauren was pregnant, that's what was wrong. He should have told her, dammit. Told her they could never have kids. Make that a condition of them being together, being a couple.

Hey, Lauren, wanna marry me? Only thing is, we can't have kids. If you're not down with that, forget it.

Who the fuck was he kidding?

He'd walk barefoot across broken glass to be with Lauren.

Just no kids.

But…here she was, expecting.

Fuck.

How could she have a kid with *him* when he had no freaking *clue* who he came from? The only thing he knew was that his heritage wasn't good, any of it.

Mom a junkie and dad some passing drunk.

Genes counted for something, didn't they?

Jacko looked up at the gray, low sky. Cold rain fell on his upturned face, but it didn't cool him. He felt hot, like he was bursting into flame.

Lauren bleeding to death flashed across his vision again and bile rose up his gullet. He leaned forward and vomited last night's dinner. His stomach simply emptied itself out, the contents splashing onto the shoulder of the road in great heaving spasms. He had no control, none.

His body was rejecting what was in his stomach and rejecting the thought of Lauren pregnant with his child.

He dry heaved for a while even after there was nothing left in his stomach except the lining. Finally he put his hand on the fender to hold himself up and stared at the ground. Nothing to see, really, except gravel, puddles and vomit. He couldn't move, though. His legs wouldn't carry him.

Finally, finally, he straightened up and got back into the cab of the vehicle, moving like an old man.

Jacko was a fast driver, but driving fast was out of the question. He didn't have the coordination. He made it to the Pearl and headed toward the gate. His company, ASI, had a transponder system that opened the gates fast when an ASI transponder was within a hundred feet. He loved racing up to the gates, knowing they'd open at the last minute, and roaring into the parking area of his company.

Now he waited for the gates to open and drove slowly in, clutching the steering wheel with sweaty palms. He was being recorded by the security cams and whoever was on oversight wouldn't recognize his driving.

Inside the company the atmosphere was busy but calm, as it always was. Jacko loved the company, loved working there. He felt a big rush every time he walked into the big command-and-control area designed by Suzanne Huntington, the wife of one of his bosses, John Huntington. The Midnight Man.

But today he didn't feel anything except numb. He headed toward his desk to add to the file he'd already sent from Tijuana, finish up the details of his report, but his legs wouldn't carry him to his desk. Instead, he went straight for Felicity, their IT genius, the fiancée of one of his best friends, Metal O'Brien.

Jacko didn't know he was going to do this, but his body did.

He had read once about a guy who'd gone crazy and said his body disconnected from his head. Jacko remembered thinking *bullshit*. That doesn't happen. You tell your body what to do. But here he was, with his body in the driver's seat and his head just along for the ride.

Felicity was, as usual, pounding on her magic computer that no one else was allowed to touch. To even breathe on.

He waited for a lull in the typing and reached out to touch her shoulder.

"Hey, Jacko," Felicity said without glancing away from her monitor. Word had it her computer had 360° situational awareness.

Jacko moved quietly. She couldn't have heard him coming. "How'd you know it was me?"

Felicity twisted her head around and smiled at him. She was very pretty, though not in Lauren's league. He was aware that Metal thought the same of Lauren.

She gave a little laugh. Laughter was something new for Felicity. She'd had it rough in the past and she'd entered Metal's life by falling wounded and bleeding across the threshold of Lauren's front door. Now she laughed a lot. Metal had given that to her.

She swiveled her chair around and looked up at him. "I'd like to say I'm all-seeing—and I *am* all-knowing—but the truth is that I saw your reflection in the monitor." She looked closer at him and frowned. "Jacko? Something wrong? You look really…tired."

So she'd picked up on something. Not hard, since he was sweating and shifting his weight from boot to boot.

Jacko nodded to the back wall, where a door led to a quiet corridor. "Can we go to the SCIF?" Pronounced skiff. Secure Compartmented Information Facility. A high-tech room shielded from any kind of surveillance. ASI did business with a lot of three- letter government agencies, and sometimes the briefings were ultra top secret. The government had to know the intel was going to stay inside ASI. "And can you take Puff the Magic Dragon with you?"

"Sure." Felicity didn't miss a beat. She rose, cup of coffee in one hand and Puff, her computer, in the other.

Nobody gave them a second glance as they walked out of the big control room and into the quiet corridor. The third door to the right had a keypad and Felicity entered the code. She was probably the one at ASI who used the facility the most. Government agencies vied for her services. They'd also tried to hire her away tons of times but she wasn't interested. As long as Metal was here, she was here. And like Jacko, she loved working for ASI.

The air of the SCIF felt dead. There were no windows and the walls and the door were metal-clad. They sat down at the conference table under a glass umbrella and Felicity brought out Puff. SCIFs were air-gapped, no-internet zones—no info went in and none went out. But Felicity could go on the net with Puff with no adverse consequences.

Felicity was scary sometimes.

She placed her hand on the matte silvery-gray surface of her laptop and waited for Jacko to tell her what this was about. Confidential briefings were nothing new for her.

Jacko swallowed. This wasn't business and it was fucking hard.

He looked Felicity in the eye, then glanced away. "You're used to keeping secrets." It was a statement.

She nodded. "My blood is Russian," she said calmly. "We keep secrets for generations."

Yeah. Felicity had grown up in the Witness Protection Program. She'd had three names before the age of twenty. She knew how to keep secrets.

Jacko met her eyes. "Lauren's pregnant."

Felicity didn't blink. "Congratulations. I'm not hearing happiness, though."

He couldn't talk, simply couldn't get anything past his throat. She didn't fill the air with chatter, just sat in silence with him.

Finally, Jacko dropped his gaze. "I'm glad. I think. But…" He waited until the boulder sitting on his chest shifted enough to get words out. "I never knew my father. Never even knew who he was. My mom never told me. I think she didn't know either. She was a drug addict and there were a lot of men passing through her bed."

Felicity didn't change expression. Her light blue eyes were friendly and calm. The lack of reaction helped him get the rest of it out.

"My mom was troubled." He shrugged. "She was a junkie. They *are* the definition of trouble. I don't know much about her. I don't even know who her parents—my grandparents—were. She never told me, never talked about them. That never bothered me until Lauren told me she was expecting. My mom's blood and my father's blood will flow through the child's veins. And that scares me shitless. I'm okay. I know I have my faults—"

"You sure do," Felicity said. "You're a real sore loser."

"Yeah." He and his ASI buddies had rolling poker games, and he always lost to Joe Harris and he hated it. He hated losing. "I am."

"I don't think that's hereditary," she said.

"But a lot of other bad shit is," he answered.

The tips of her fingers ran over the laptop cover as she nodded. "What can I do to help, Jacko?"

Jacko blew out a silent breath. "Find her. Find out who my mother was. Who she came from. Can you do that for me?" It wouldn't be easy. Jacko knew nothing about her life. "No matter what you find, knowing is better than not knowing."

Felicity opened the laptop and Jacko could swear the air shimmered above the keyboard. She poised her fingers over the keys. "Let's start with what you do know. When did she die and where?"

"She died either the 8th or 9th of October, 2000. She died while I was in BUD/S. During Hell Week. The instructors knew we weren't close. A lotta guys in my class weren't close to their folks. A couple had something like my situation back home. The instructors knew the Navy was our family. They waited until I passed BUD/S and then told me. They said it took the authorities a couple of days to track me down. So that would put it at the 8th or 9th."

"You never saw the death certificate?"

Jacko shook his head. "Nope. Never even occurred to me to ask to see it. It certainly wasn't offered. I hadn't spoken to since I left to join the Navy."

Felicity didn't react in any way. "So what was her name and where did she pass away?"

"Sara Jackman. Cross, Texas."

Her fingers started blurring. He had no idea how she could work that fast, but she did. Almost immediately, she halted. "Okay, this is what I have on the death certificate. Your mom was born in Rancho San Diego, California. Jackman was her married name, she was born Sara Garrett. Her parents were Lee and Alice Garrett."

"Wait." Jacko pinched the bridge of his nose. "She was married? Jackman was her *married name*?" He'd had no idea she'd been married. She never talked about it at all. Of course she rarely talked to him about anything, particularly those last years when her brain had gone up in smoke. "This Jackman—was he…was he my father?"

Was it going to be this easy?

Felicity looked at him. "You didn't know she was married?"

"Hell no. My mom could barely lurch from day to day there at the end and I was in and out of foster homes. She never spoke about her past. Like I said, I have no idea who her parents were. They can't have been good parents if she was such a mess."

"When were you born, Jacko, and where?" Felicity was frowning at the screen, waiting.

"I was born March 6, 1980, in Cross, Texas." The most miserable hole in the state. If Texas ever needed an enema, Cross is where they'd give it.

She was silent for a couple of minutes as she worked furiously, then sat back. One last command and she pulled up data on her screen.

"Sara Garrett married Robert Jackman in 1977, and he died in 1978, so no, he couldn't have been your father. She never divorced and kept the name." Felicity looked at him soberly. "Jacko...your grandfather died very recently. Six months ago, actually."

Whoa. He'd had a grandfather alive all this time? "Jesus."

"His wife, your grandmother, died fifteen years earlier. From what I can see, your grandfather was a respected member of the community. Certainly no legal issues. Grandmother, too. Your mom, on the other hand..." she hesitated.

"Was in and out of jail," Jacko said bleakly. "For possession and solicitation. In and out of rehab. I know. I was taken away from her a bunch of times and put in foster homes. She'd do a little time, get out on good behavior, get me back, start collecting child support checks and go right back to chasing the next high. I learned long ago there was no saving her. I guess I always thought she came from bad genes herself."

"Not necessarily." Felicity frowned at the screen. "It's hard to tell. Official data won't give info on private behavior. Your grandfather might have been abusive, who knows? Yet he seemed to be well respected. He was given a few civic awards. Hmm. He must have had some money, too. There were a series of park benches donated in his wife's name the year after she died. He had a huge ranch, though land lots have been sold off the last fifteen years." She met Jacko's eyes. "He died leaving everything to his daughter, 'whereabouts unknown.' Jacko, you're her only heir, that ranch is yours."

She turned the screen around so he could see the address and phone numbers of a law firm. She pressed a key and a secure printer started whirring. "That's the law office that handled Lee Garrett's affairs, I'm printing the info now."

Jacko pulled the sheets and clutched them in his hand. He had an excellent memory and normally he wouldn't need to keep the written info, but he was still reeling from the fact that he'd had a grandfather all along and hadn't known it.

He scanned the printouts but they were a blur. He couldn't seem to take in any of the info. He leaned in. "Do—do you have images for him?"

"Yeah." She did that finger-blurring thing again, then sat back. The monitor showed a carousel of photographs and Jacko stared. They were mainly informal snapshots, some formal portraits, some cuttings from newspapers. Lee Garrett smiling into the lens, growing more unsmiling as he aged. Being handed some kind of award. With a hunting rifle, in hunting gear, one booted foot on the neck of a six-point buck. Standing next to a big Christmas tree. Several shots at restaurants. He'd been a member of the Rotary Club and there were lots of photos at Rotary dinners.

Jacko took in all the details greedily, but there was nothing there to hang on to. Garrett was tall, lanky, fair-skinned, with a full head of sandy hair. He had nothing in common with Jacko's strong, stout build and dark skin. However hard Jacko looked, he could see no points of resemblance. Nothing.

His wife, too, was tall and slender. Attractive without making much of an effort. There were a couple of shots of her on a hunting trip, holding a shotgun as if she knew how to use it. There were no photographs of her much beyond the age of forty. Felicity said she died fifteen years ago. Felicity had included her birth date—1951. She died at 50.

He watched in a daze as the photos crossed the screen, and then— "Stop."

Felicity obediently stopped the carousel of photos.

A family snapshot. Lee, his wife, a young girl standing between them, face scrunched up against the sun.

Jesus. His mother. Looking…normal. Like any other teenager in the '70s. Peering closely, Jacko could vaguely see his mother in the teenager's face. The last years he'd seen his mother, she'd been grossly underweight, face heavily lined, prematurely gray hair falling out in clumps. Teeth ground down to black stubs because of the meth. She looked like shit, always. None too clean and on the lookout for the next high, no matter the price.

This girl looked happy and energetic.

There she was, in another photo, happily holding up a sports trophy. And another, on a horse in English riding gear. And another one, in a cheerleader's outfit.

What the fuck had happened to her?

There were no photographs of the girl after her late teens. She disappeared from the Garretts' lives. Alice Garrett aged ten years in each photo and then she, too, disappeared. Only Lee Garrett remained, looking older and sadder and more stooped in each shot.

Jacko knew he'd just watched the breakdown of a family, and that was too bad, but he felt absolutely nothing. The faces meant nothing to him and his mother as a young girl was so unlike the woman he remembered, it was as if they were two different people.

He studied Lee and Alice Garrett again, searching deep inside himself for some spark of recognition, but got absolutely nothing. They were two faces out of the 260 million adults in the US. He wouldn't believe they had anything to do with him if he hadn't recognized his mother. Barely.

Wow. So what now?

"You know, Jacko," Felicity said gently. "Maybe you might want to contact that lawyer. From what I gather, the house and property are there, waiting for an heir. At some point, everything will revert back to the state."

Jacko stiffened. "I don't need his money." Fuck no. He was doing just fine. He'd saved a lot while in the Navy and ASI paid really well. And Lauren had inherited money from her mother and was earning more with her art. He didn't need anybody's money.

"Not for the money. But because in that house, there might be some stuff that will tell you what you need to know. I understand you're okay with your past but surely more information would be…helpful?"

Damn right he was okay with his past, for the simple reason that he never ever thought about it. It was not a problem, no sir.

Except for right now, with Lauren pregnant. He needed to be okay with this because he was not going to lose Lauren, and he was going to be a good father. If it killed him, which it might.

Maybe Felicity was right. Maybe some more intel would be good.

"Here, Jacko." Felicity pulled a flash drive he hadn't even seen from the side of Puff the Magic Dragon and handed it to him. He turned it over in his hand. It was tiny, and knowing Felicity, it wasn't available on the market and it could probably contain files the size of the NSA's. "All this info, including photos, is on this drive. I also sent most of the pertinent data to your cell. Call the lawyer. See what he says. Maybe when you have time, go down and see the house." She paused a beat, looking carefully at his face. "What have you got to lose?"

Because he couldn't be doing worse than he was now, was the unspoken message. Jacko had gotten a glimpse of himself in a mirror and he looked like shit. Pale beneath his dark skin, deep purple bags under his eyes. He never looked like this. He had huge reserves. It took weeks of hard work or being on an op for him to even start to get tired.

Right now he was exhausted, wrung out.

And he was failing Lauren.

His shit was getting in the way of her happiness. She didn't deserve this. She deserved a man who was whole.

Not a man who vomited at the thought of fatherhood.

For a guy who planned his every move in advance, Jacko hadn't the faintest idea what came next. He only knew he had to take that first step toward finding out where he came from.

He swallowed heavily. "If I go…somewhere, make sure Lauren doesn't worry. Make sure she's okay."

Even more bullshit from Mr. Straight Talk.

But Felicity understood a lot of what he wasn't saying. She was smart, and she knew about secrets and the holes they dug in lives. Her parents had kept secrets all her life. She knew what this was like.

"Don't worry about Lauren. We'll all look after her." Felicity nodded, stood up.

"I'm turning the transponder off." The words were out before he could block them. All ASI vehicles had a transponder. Nobody ever turned theirs off. Why would they? But Jacko needed to go out on his own, without the connection to ASI. He didn't want to be followed until he knew what he would uncover.

Felicity nodded soberly. "All right." She had no expression on her face at all. "We okay here?"

"Yeah. And thanks."

She put a hand on his shoulder, squeezed lightly and walked out.

Jacko sat in the super-quiet room a long time, thinking. Finally, he stood up and made his way to a lounge area that was usually empty during the working day. ASI employees gathered there when they worked late or had to work on weekends. It was always stocked with food and water and coffee.

Jacko didn't want food. His stomach rose halfway up his gullet at the idea. But he did want some coffee and he wanted solitude.

He entered the lounge and, after a moment's hesitation, locked the door. The door was never locked but right now he needed to be on his own. There wasn't any bandwidth in him to talk to anyone.

He poured himself a big mug of coffee and downed it black, not tasting it. Not even feeling it. Then he scrolled through his cell until he had the lawyer's name.

Ernest Mayer, Llc. Head of his own law firm. Three landlines and a cell, all with the same 619 prefix.

Jacko cradled the cell in the palm of his hand and stared at it, the plastic warming up while the coffee cooled down.

Do the hard thing. The SEAL mantra.

He dialed the cell number and waited. A man answered with a single word. "Mayer."

Jacko waited, a tight knot in his throat, his stomach balled up tight. Until he spoke, the machine wouldn't be set in motion. But that was a lie. The machine was set in motion the second Lauren told him she was pregnant.

"Hello? Who is this?" The soft, cultivated male voice was impatient.

"Mr. Mayer, my name is Morton Jackman." As always, his first name came out sounding strange. Morton was always for the most formal of occasions. When he signed official documents, the "Morton" was in a different hand. He never used it.

"What can I do for you, Mr. Jackman?"

"I understand you were the lawyer of Lee Garrett."

"Yes, I was. Now I represent his estate." A brief pause. "May I ask what this is about?"

Jacko clenched his jaw so hard his teeth ground together. "I'm the son of Sara Jackman."

"I don't know any Sara Jackman. I'm sorry, but—"

"You would have known her as Sara Garrett. Lee Garrett's daughter."

There was complete silence.

"Mr. Mayer?"

"I—yes. This is—this is incredible news. Sara Garrett ran away from home thirty-seven years ago and was never seen again." He paused. "I am going to need proof, sir."

"Mr. Mayer, I am sending you my birth certificate, my mother's marriage certificate, the death certificate of her husband, Robert Jackman, her death certificate, and a copy of my passport."

Jacko heard a faint ping. "I received the documents, Mr. Jackman. Please give me a moment to look at them." The voice quavered and for the first time, Jacko realized he was an old man. He must have been Lee Garrett's contemporary. Garrett had been over seventy years old when he passed away. "If these documents are valid, then you are the sole heir to Lee Garrett's estate. It is considerable. There's a home with several acres attached, close to a million dollars in investments, a—"

"I'm not interested in the estate, per se," Jacko interrupted. "But I would like very much to see the house. Read any papers, documents Mr. Garrett—my grandfather—might have kept."

His voice nearly choked on the word "grandfather".

"Mr. Jackman. If what you're saying is corroborated, then of course you can have full access to Lee Garrett's home, his papers, anything you want. It will take time to process everything, but the estate will be yours. Lee—Mr. Garrett—left all of his assets to his daughter. If she is deceased, it all goes to you. I don't know where you are, Mr. Jackman—"

"I live in Portland, Oregon," Jacko said.

"If you could possibly plan a trip down south, at your convenience, we could start the paperwork for transferring the estate to you."

Jacko was suddenly burning to get to old man Garrett's house, start looking through his stuff, start getting fucking *answers*. Normally a patient man, a man who could lie in a sniper's nest for days for a chance at a shot, he was feverish with hurry. He checked his watch and then the map in his head. "I'd like to drive down right away. What are your office hours?"

Silence. "It's a long drive down, Mr. Jackman," the lawyer answered, deep emotion shaking his voice. "You'll probably arrive late Saturday evening or early Sunday morning. But I will come in for you at any time. Lee Garrett was one of my closest friends. I would do anything for his grandson. Call me when you have an estimated time of arrival. I will wait for you, Mr. Jackman, for as long as it takes."

"I'm on my way," Jacko said and clicked off.

He was tunnel-visioning, almost incapable of seeing or thinking of anything but the drive down to Rancho San Diego, getting to the home of a man who, improbably, might be his grandfather.

But some vestige of something—some sense of duty—made him stop by Metal's desk. Metal was in the middle of planning the logistics of a bug-out encampment for a small company. ASI's newest growth market was planning for when the shit hit the fan. An amazingly large number of people thought the apocalypse was coming in one form or another, and wanted to plan for survival.

ASI was planning its own survival encampment. Metal was the resident expert, with Jacko advising.

He was totally into the plan for the small company, nose an inch from his screen. Jacko tapped him on the shoulder. "Yo, bro."

Metal sat up, shook his head as if just coming back from a long dive, turned around. He frowned. "Hey, man, you look like shit." The exact same thing Felicity had said, only she'd said it more gently.

"I've got some personal time coming," Jacko said. "I'm taking it now."

He turned his whole body into a "don't mess with me" zone. Jacko was good at that. He was an alpha male and was good at intimidating. But Metal was an alpha male, too. Metal stood up and got right in Jacko's grill.

"You do have personal time coming, a lot of it. But right now is not a good time. We have the Ferrago contract coming up and—"

"Metal. Honey." Felicity suddenly appeared at Metal's side, a pretty hand on Metal's big shoulder. "Jacko really does need the time off. He won't be long, will you, Jacko?"

Jacko shook his head.

Metal shut up, but he had a big scowl on his face. Felicity had let him know he shouldn't pursue this, and whatever Felicity wanted, she got. But Metal wasn't happy about it and he was showing it.

Metal was his closest friend. If it were anything else, Jacko would have talked it over with him. Planned it, maybe. Taken time off when the company had a down moment, though those were rare. ASI was a fair company and if he gave notice, they'd work around his needs. Him suddenly disappearing like this wasn't fair to the company.

He hated that. He hated not being able to talk to his best friend.

But the truth was—he couldn't. He was vibrating inside. His throat was hot and tight. There was no way words could get out, even if he had words to explain what was going on, which he didn't.

This was bad. All of it was bad. Lauren having a baby that was half his was *really* bad.

He couldn't talk about it, any of it.

Jacko turned on his heel and left.

When the back employee door closed behind him, Jacko stood in the chilly air. He knew it was cold but the cold never affected him. And right now? He felt like a nuclear reactor. Unfortunately, one about ready to blow.

In his SUV, he drummed his fingers on the wheel. He had a go-bag in the back. He was always prepared. The go-bag had several changes of clothes, a basic toiletry kit and a very well-stocked medical kit. It also had about four thousand dollars in cash, a Glock 19 and a Sig Sauer P320 with a thousand rounds of ammo.

Besides the go-bag, there was an M24 sniper rifle in its case, a pup tent and sleeping bag, several cases of water and enough MREs to survive several days.

Because you never know.

The gates to the ASI compound opened and Jacko drove through and then stopped in the driving rain. He usually turned right, toward home. He should stop by the house, explain things to Lauren. She worried about him when he was out of town. She worried about him in general, fussing when he wasn't eating properly, wasn't dressed warmly enough, wasn't getting enough sleep.

She loved him.

He had to swing by, tell her he was leaving for a few days.

North was home. South was California, and maybe Texas.

North was home and love. South was his painful past.

The rain swept a lash of water over the windshield so strong it overwhelmed even the SUV's powerful wipers.

Jacko pulled out and turned left. South.

CHAPTER THREE

Lauren worried. Jacko was supposed to be home in the early afternoon. She'd been waiting for his call to say he was coming home but hadn't heard anything at all. The celebratory dinner was almost ready. She had the roast in the oven and the house was filled with mouthwatering scents. They only made her stomach clench.

Wasn't it early for morning sickness? Evening sickness, in this case.

In her heart, she knew she wasn't nauseous because of the pregnancy. She was frightened of Jacko's reaction. Nothing much shook him, but the news that they were expecting a baby seemed to have bowled him over.

And yet they had so much sex, it was a miracle she hadn't become pregnant before this.

A wave of heat shot through her as she thought of their sex life. For the two years she'd been on the run from her murderous step-cousin, she hadn't had sex at all. And even before then…well, she'd always been kind of picky. She had more sex in a week with Jacko than in the previous decade. She couldn't even remember sex with other men, though she had had a few boyfriends in college. They were wiped from her mind, as if they had never existed.

Sometimes she thought Jacko was imprinted on her. She spent so much time in his arms, her skin sweaty with the heat of sex, she thought it was a miracle his tribal tattoos didn't transfer themselves to her skin.

She was sitting on the couch, having given up any pretense of work. No way could she settle down and work while waiting for Jacko, unsure of his reaction.

She had a monthly shot but it couldn't possibly be a bulwark against the kind of sex she had with Jacko. Long, intense, endless. No shot of chemicals in the world could counteract all that sperm. Some nights her whole groin was wet with their juices.

She fingered a cushion as another flash of heat shot through her. The night before Jacko left for Mexico, they'd made love right here, on this couch. They hadn't even made it to the bedroom. That look she'd come to recognize so intimately had flashed across his dark face and the next thing she knew, they were both naked and he was buried in her, thrusting hard…

Lauren tilted her head back and closed her eyes. Wanting her lover with every fiber of her being.

They had no barriers between them. She loved that. Loved that they were so attuned to each other. That stiffness this morning between them broke her heart. She couldn't stand it, not one second more. When he came home they'd have it out, though if he didn't want the child—

If he didn't want the child, what was she going to do? Because she *did* want it. Her hand curled over her stomach. It was still flat. According to the billion articles she'd read on the internet, their child was still basically just some cells, multiplying furiously. But she loved it already and nothing on this earth would keep her from it.

If Jacko didn't want this baby, there was no compromise possible. She wasn't aborting, she wasn't going to give it up for adoption, this baby was hers. She loved it. She loved Jacko. If she couldn't have both…

The doorbell rang and her eyes popped open. Jacko didn't ring the doorbell. He just entered, quiet as a panther. Who could it possibly be at this hour?

Felicity, Isabel and Summer. That's who. She stared at her friends on the wall panel and hesitated just a second before pressing the button that would open the door.

She loved her friends. Seeing them at her door under ordinary circumstances would fill her with happiness, because she'd know for a fact that laughter and probably excellent cake supplied by Isabel would follow.

But not tonight. Tonight she and Jacko had things to thrash out.

But they were here and they loved her so she pressed the button.

"Surprise!" Felicity came in first, kissing her cheek. "We bring gifts. Or rather, Isabel brings gifts. You wouldn't want my cooking."

"Or mine." Summer Delvaux, married to Isabel's brother, stepped into the room and kissed her. She shuddered. "Jack complains all the time about my cooking. Lucky thing Isabel lives so close."

Isabel brought up the rear, holding a tinfoil-covered pan to one side as she kissed Lauren's cheek, too. "Double chocolate fudge. Pure evil sin. We're definitely going to hell, but not before having a really good time."

Lauren forced herself to smile as she shut the door behind them. She checked the time on the ormolu clock on the mantle that had belonged to her great-grandmother. 8:00 p.m. Jacko was late. He was never late without calling, which meant he'd be coming home any second now. He enjoyed the company of Felicity, Isabel and Summer. Metal was his best friend. Isabel's guy, Joe Harris, was another good friend. Joe and Metal and Jacko had served together as SEALs. Summer's love, Jack

Delvaux, Isabel's brother, was a recent addition to ASI.

They all hung out together a lot and always had a really good time.

But not tonight.

Felicity, Isabel and Summer were making themselves at home. They knew where to hang the coats and made a beeline for the kitchen. They stopped on the threshold when they saw the small dining room just off the kitchen. The table was set for an occasion with a lace tablecloth and Lauren's best china. Two tall candles in crystal candleholders were just waiting to be lit.

"Ah, ladies?" Lauren gave a weak smile. "I'm delighted to see you, and Isabel? That fudge is not leaving this house, but tonight isn't the best of evenings to get together. I'm having, um, a special dinner with Jacko."

Felicity turned and caught Lauren's hands. She was taller than Lauren so when she bent forward to give her a hug, Lauren fit against her shoulder.

"Honey…" Felicity looked at Isabel and Summer, then back at her. "That's why we're here. There's no easy way to say this, so I'll just come right out with it. I don't think Jacko is coming home."

Her head swam. Lauren shot out a hand to steady herself, but she found herself held upright by her friends.

"*Ever?*" Lauren whispered, shocked to her toes. Her knees trembled.

Isabel and Summer held her, made her sit down on one of the dining table chairs. Summer gently pushed the nape of her neck down between her knees. "Breathe," Summer said calmly.

Lauren barely heard her. Jacko wasn't coming home? He was *leaving* her? She tried to imagine a universe in which Jacko left her, but she couldn't.

She lifted her head in time to see Isabel roll her eyes at Felicity. "Way to go, Felicity. Don't mind her, honey. She's a nerd, hopeless around humans."

"Yes, I am. I'm really sorry to give you a shock." Felicity hung her head, long blonde ponytail hanging to the side of her face. "And Jacko is not leaving you. I don't think he knows how to leave you. But he *has* gone away. For a little while."

Lauren's head was still whirling. Nothing made sense.

Summer stuck her head in the fridge. "This situation calls for Prosecco and fudge, stat." She pulled out a bottle of Prosecco Lauren had been keeping for Jacko. Jacko disliked champagne but loved Prosecco, go figure.

"Not for me," she said.

"Not for Lauren," Felicity said at the same time.

Summer stopped, bottle in hand, and looked between the two of them. She was super-smart and put it together in a flash. "You're pregnant," she said to Lauren.

God. Summer was a Pulitzer Prize-winning investigative journalist. She'd uncovered the conspiracy behind the Washington Massacre. One pregnancy—even if just a few cells along—was nothing to her eagle eyes.

"Barely." Lauren sighed. "Barely pregnant."

"No such thing as barely pregnant." Isabel sat down beside her and took her hand. "How far along are you?"

"Far enough along to avoid alcohol. And you guys weren't supposed to know for a while."

"Nothing escapes us," Summer said smugly, taking the dinner plates off the table and setting it with dessert plates. Isabel placed the big pan of fudge on the table and started cutting squares. "We are all-knowing and all-seeing."

"And we have brought the panacea for all ailments. Chocolate." Isabel started serving, giving Lauren an extra-large portion.

Lauren was worried sick about Jacko, but the large square of luscious-looking dark chocolate on her rose-covered dessert plates took a little of the edge off the anxiety. She was about to say so when her cell rang.

She rushed to pick it up. The breath whooshed out of her lungs when she saw who was calling. Jacko. Thank God.

She moved quietly into the bedroom for privacy. The girls were busy with the fudge, but looked up curiously when she moved away. She looked at them fondly, Isabel, Felicity and Summer, each with a bite of fudge speared on a dessert fork. They cared for her and she cared for them, but right now, she needed to talk to Jacko like she needed air.

Closing the bedroom door, she clicked the connection. "Jacko? Darling, I'm so glad to hear your voice. Why aren't you home?"

There was nothing but silence on the other end.

Lauren pressed the cell harder against her ear. She could make out the faint sound of breathing. Jacko's breathing was like everything about him—strong and steady. But this sounded ragged, stressed.

"Darling?"

Silence. But she could almost hear him listening on the other end. She had no idea where he was but could picture him, listening hard, unable to speak.

For an instant it scared her—Jacko unable to speak. Jacko could do anything. He was the strongest, most capable man she'd ever met.

But this wasn't about her and her fear of losing him. It was about Jacko. To behave like this—totally unlike him—must mean he was hurting badly.

Lauren turned on her bedside lamp and sat down on her side of the bed. She placed a hand on the mattress for balance as she sat, then curved the hand over her belly.

How many times had they made love on this bed? This was probably where they conceived the child that lay under her hand.

She loved them both so much. The child and the man.

"Jacko?"

When he didn't answer, she began speaking.

"I don't know where you are, darling. I hope you're well. I had a nice dinner all planned for us, to—to celebrate. I know the news of our child upset you, somehow. I don't pretend to understand it, but I respect it. It's hard—dealing with the thought of becoming a mother or a father. Maybe it's easier for me because I had a little more time to get used to it. And I can feel it—him or her. He or she is tiny still, but I can feel something growing inside me. I think in time you'll get used to the idea. There's so much love inside you, Jacko. I know you're surprised at how much you love me. You've told me that so many times. And I wonder if you feel you only have room for one in your heart. But—I don't think it works like that, you know? I think the heart expands. You've got a big heart, my darling. A big, strong heart. There's room for both of us inside."

She stopped because the tears she didn't want to shed could be heard in her voice. Whatever was going on inside Jacko was a battle only he could fight. She didn't want to add to his burden. But she did want him to know she loved him.

"I know that because I know there's room in *my* heart for you and our baby. And maybe more babies to come. Who knows?"

Her voice wobbled and she covered her face with her hand.

They sat listening to each other breathing, connected only via radio waves and by their hearts and the love they had for each other.

"Felicity, Isabel and Summer are over. They're in the kitchen right now and I suspect they might end up eating the dinner I prepared for us. That's okay. It's just food. I'll prepare another nice meal for when you come home."

More silence.

Lauren refused to think of Jacko not ever coming home again. It was unthinkable.

"When you come back, we'll celebrate, won't we, darling? Because it's something to celebrate. We made a new life together, you and me. A child. A boy or a girl who will grow up loved, healthy and happy. You've worked so hard to make the world a safer place. We'll work hard together to give the world someone better. Did you know Isabel and Joe are talking about having kids? And Isabel is trying to get Summer and Jack to think of having kids, too. Jack is all for it, Summer said. But then Isabel and Jack grew up in an amazing family. Summer—not so much. It's hard if you haven't grown up in a happy family. I didn't, and God knows you didn't either. You haven't said much about your mom, but it's enough to understand you had it rough. Our child won't have it rough. We'll love her, or him. Our child will grow up with Isabel and Joe's kids, and maybe Summer and Jack's kids. Like cousins."

In the silence, sounds from the kitchen filtered through.

"I'm going to hang up now, darling. I need to get back to the girls before they finish the amazing fudge Isabel brought. Wherever you are, I love you." She waited a minute until her voice steadied. "Come home to me, Jacko. Come home to us."

She clicked off and sat, head bowed, until her hands stopped trembling and she could take a deep breath without choking.

Back in the kitchen, she nearly laughed at the tableau. Three women looked up guiltily. Half the pan of fudge was gone, as was the bottle of Prosecco.

"Here," Isabel said, putting a saucer and cup on the table. She produced a teapot she'd taken from Lauren's cupboard. "I made you some tea. Ginger and lemon in case you're having trouble digesting."

"Thanks." Lauren dredged up a credible smile and sat down. The tea was still hot and delicious, and settled her stomach. "I'm glad you guys left me a little chocolate."

Felicity hesitated, then put her long hand over Lauren's. "That was Jacko, wasn't it?"

All three looked at her, concern in their eyes.

"Yes." Lauren coughed to loosen her throat. "It was."

"It'll be okay. I think he needs some time, that's all." Felicity was known for her straight talk. She didn't sugarcoat anything.

"Yes." Suddenly, Lauren straightened up, sat taller. She was with her three best friends in the world. Her child was going to grow up with them, consider them aunts. Her child was going to grow up with two loving parents, surrounded by loving adults. "Jacko will be back as soon as he's done what he needs to do."

All three nodded soberly.

"He'll be back." Lauren believed that with all her heart.

"Absolutely." Summer pushed a plate of fudge to her. "Have some chocolate."

Jacko had driven the Portland–San Diego route many times along the Pacific Coast Highway. It was a beautiful drive, but slow. Now he wanted to arrow down and across to Rancho San Diego as fast as possible.

He could fly. But he'd have to wait until tomorrow, book a ticket on the first flight, rent a car…

No. Not while he felt like he was jumping out of his skin. He had to get going *now*. It was going to be a long, long drive, but he didn't care. He needed to be alone and he needed to think, so he took the I-5 and settled in.

But first he'd had to talk to Lauren. He couldn't just disappear on her. She'd be worried and that felt like broken glass under his skin. The thought of making Lauren unhappy, worried, because of him—he couldn't go there. Couldn't do it.

But the thing was—he'd already done it. He hadn't gone home, to the dinner she prepared. He knew what her special dinners were like. She brought out her best everything, prepared an extra-nice meal. She'd have set the tables with candles. She'd have made a fuss over the food. She loved it.

He loved it.

No one had ever made a special occasion for him. Somehow Lauren understood that and so she celebrated everything it was possible to celebrate. Birthdays, promotions, when he came home from a road trip. Christmas, Easter, Labor Day, Memorial Day, the fourth of July…she did it all, because she knew how much he loved it.

So she'd prepared a special meal tonight so they could celebrate the fact that she was expecting their child.

Jacko swallowed what felt like stones.

Jesus.

He'd just skipped out on her. Disappeared, like some lowlife. Like the guys who fucked his mom and then left.

He wasn't any different. The fact that he loved Lauren didn't make him any better than they were. Made him worse than they were because she expected more from him.

All he had to do was turn around. He was near Crater Lake. Just call up, say he'd had a work thing, would be home a little late, and she'd forgive him. She always did. Never even complained.

He could do that right now. Call up and say— I'm coming home.

Jacko swerved to the side of the road and parked in a lay-by. He dialed and after two rings, she picked up.

He closed his eyes when he heard her soft voice asking where he was.

Away, he wanted to answer. *I'm away from you and I don't want to be. I'm coming home.*

But he didn't.

He didn't say anything. For the life of him, he couldn't get anything out at all. His throat burned, he couldn't push air out, couldn't do anything but listen to her talking to him, gently and with love.

She understood. He didn't know what she understood. He didn't understand too much himself. Since when couldn't he even fucking talk? But she got it that something was happening and she wasn't mad at him, which was a miracle. She was sad, though.

Yeah, what the hell did he expect? That she'd be happy he was behaving like an asshole?

At least she wasn't alone. Felicity, Isabel and Summer were with her. And that meant that Metal, Joe and Jack would be watching over her, too. He was lucky that he had people in his life who'd look after Lauren, who cared about her.

And about him, too.

Speaking of which—he picked up his cell after Lauren hung up and tapped a number.

Metal. Not happy.

"Dude, the fuck are you doing?"

Jacko didn't have any trouble talking to Metal. His throat didn't seize up. He could talk just fine.

"Gotta do this."

"Gotta do *what?* Leave Lauren while she's expecting? Just pick up and go when you hear you're going to be a dad? What kind of fuckhead does that?"

Jacko's jaw clenched. The guys at ASI and their women had this internal intel machine that was amazing. Everybody knew everything at once. He was sure Felicity hadn't talked, but then she didn't have to. Women had sixth senses about things like love affairs and pregnancies. And the women talked to their men.

Jacko didn't have time for this.

"I won't be gone more than a few days. Look after Lauren for me." He closed the connection and turned his cell off. He'd talked to everyone he needed to. Lauren and one of the guys.

Well, he hadn't *talked* talked to Lauren, but they'd communicated, in a half-assed way. And he'd told Metal to take care of Lauren, knowing that meant Joe and Jack and his bosses, John Huntington and his former senior chief, Douglas Kowalski, would be there if Lauren needed anything. Their wives, too. Suzanne and Allegra.

Lauren had a tribe to look after her while Jacko went out and did what he had to do.

He pulled out onto the Interstate, propelled by forces stronger than he was. Forces that had begun before his birth. Forces not even his love for Lauren could deny.

He pressed on the accelerator, continuing his journey south.

CHAPTER FOUR

Men trooped in and out of the house all day. It started with one of Jacko's two bosses, Douglas Kowalski. He stopped by in the early morning with fresh croissants from the local bakery. The croissants were not as good as the ones Isabel baked, but then she was in a class of her own.

Douglas looked as scary as Jacko, only taller and older and more scarred. But his shoulders were just as broad and his voice just as deep as Jacko's, and he gave off the same vibe. *Don't mess with me.* She'd been terrified the first time she'd seen him, just as she'd been terrified when Suzanne Huntington had sent Jacko to pick her up.

To outsiders, they were both cold-eyed warriors you'd be happy to have at your side in a fight, but would not invite to a party. Neither of them were any good at small talk.

But both of them had a totally unexpected gentle side, particularly with the ladies.

Douglas didn't step inside, though Lauren invited him in for coffee. He just handed her the bag of croissants and peeked inside from the threshold. If you found out he had X-ray vision you wouldn't be surprised, his looks were that keen.

"Anything you need?" he asked, his voice a low rumble. "Anything needs fixing?"

Lauren avoided the obvious and didn't say—*my relationship with Jacko.*

"Thanks, Douglas, but everything is in working order."

It better be. The instant something didn't work, Jacko was on it and didn't rest until it was fixed. It was like the ASI motto—*everything shall be in excellent shape.*

He looked at her fiercely, pointed a long index finger at her. "You need anything, anything at all, you call me, you hear?"

That was an order. An order by someone who had commanded Navy SEALs. It carried bite and heft. Lauren restrained herself from saluting.

"Yes, Douglas. And thank you."

His mouth firmed. She knew him pretty well by now and she was really good friends with his wife. That tight-lipped expression meant he wasn't saying what he thought. Which was that Jacko should be here.

She was grateful. She'd defend Jacko. Whatever he did was just fine in her book, and anyone who wanted to criticize him would have to go through her first. But she hadn't slept well and was feeling shaky and didn't want her voice to tremble when she took Jacko's side.

Because, well…the truth was, he *should* be here.

Douglas looked at her as if he could walk around inside her head, nodded and walked down the porch stairs and to his waiting SUV.

Lauren sagged a little. Douglas, like most of the ASI men, carried a force field around him that bent gravity a little. When they left, there was a sort of black hole that took a while to fill.

Lauren stood in the living room after he'd gone. She'd had breakfast, she'd showered, she'd made the bed. That seemed to be the extent of her planning abilities. She had work to do and ordinarily she was very self-disciplined, but today she was shaky. Had trouble getting going.

Okay. *Can't stand around forever. So what if you feel shaky? There's work to do. Your clients are expecting you to do your best for them.*

The little pep talk made her feel better. Today she'd finish the Iron Princess cover and send it off and she would start making sketches for a character in a video game. She had a feeling that would turn into another revenue generator.

The doorbell went off.

Jacko had installed a bristling array of sound and motion sensors around the house. It was a sign of her distress that she hadn't noticed the alarms for Douglas, and hadn't noticed the second person to ring her bell that morning.

Though she suspected she knew who it would be.

Either Metal O'Brien, Joe Harris, Jack Delvaux or the other ASI boss, John Huntington.

Metal. Bingo.

He was standing on her doorstep, looking fierce, holding a bag.

"Danish," he said, handing it to her. "Not as good as what Isabel makes but still."

"Thank you, Metal," she said gently. Metal was closest to Jacko and he was taking this whole thing personally.

"Anything need fixing? Anything I can do for you? Get for you?"

Lauren almost wished she could ask him to do something for her, just to make him feel better. But she didn't need anything but Jacko. And Metal couldn't do anything about that.

"Thanks, Metal. But I'm fine. Would you like a cup of coffee before going in to work?" Though it was Saturday, she knew he was going in to the office. He was working on a long-term project, something about having a place to bug out to when the zombie apocalypse hit.

"No, but thanks. Felicity's been in the office all night, working on something that came in yesterday and is time-sensitive. I need to get to her. I have more Danish in my truck."

Felicity's sweet tooth was legendary. Lauren had no idea how she stayed so slim. Probably by working so hard.

So she'd gone from Lauren's house last night—where she had spent the evening trying to make Lauren feel better—to work, working all night to make up for looking after Lauren.

Lauren felt ashamed. She was wallowing in her emotions.

She put a hand on Metal's hard shoulder and lifted up to kiss him on the cheek. Just like with the other ASI men, there was sweetness under that super-tough exterior.

"Thanks for stopping by, Metal. Give Felicity my love."

"You'll be seeing her soon." He gave her one of those looks Douglas had given her—like a welder checking a solder to make sure there were no weak spots. "If you're sure there's nothing I can do for you—"

"I'm sure," she said gently. "Thanks."

He turned and met Joe Harris coming up the walkway. Joe was carrying a cooler. They stopped, exchanged a few words—*Jacko* was one of them—and Joe carried on up to the door where Lauren stood.

Joe was as tall as Metal, but much thinner. He'd been badly wounded in battle and had only recently begun working. He'd insisted on starting work before he was ready and Lauren felt another stab of guilt.

"Hey, Lauren," he said, hefting the cooler. He was stronger than he looked. That sucker could weigh a hundred pounds, but you wouldn't know it. "Got something for you. From Isabel. I really like you, so I didn't snatch anything on the way over. Was hard, though." He cracked the cover and amazing smells came out.

"God." Knowing Isabel, there'd be enough food for an army. Or at least an ASI poker game, which might be coming up. The guys had an ongoing poker game where Joe regularly beat them. Jacko hated that, hated losing. They might organize one at her house, and the women would gather in the kitchen. They weren't going to leave her alone while Jacko was AWOL.

Tears suddenly gleamed in her eyes and Lauren panicked. She looked the other way and wiped her eyes. "Got a cold," she mumbled.

Joe shifted from foot to foot, a little embarrassed, a little angry at Jacko.

"Thank Isabel for me," she said, reaching out for the cooler. "I'll take that, unless you want a cup of coffee."

"No, I'll carry it in for you, but then I have to get going. I'll take a rain check on the coffee, thanks."

He put the cooler on the kitchen counter, bent to give her a gentle kiss on the cheek and an awkward pat on the back, and left.

Isabel looked at the cooler. Inside would be amazing things Isabel had prepared with love, but right now, Lauren's stomach was closed up tight. Though the smells were delicious, her stomach had lurched out there on the porch.

Not morning sickness. Worry.

She loved Jacko, she trusted Jacko. But the question was—did he trust himself? For him to behave like this, he had to be pushed by powerful emotions, and not good ones. Even the best of people could get pushed in bad directions by bad feelings.

Jacko would come back to her. She believed that with every fiber of her being.

But…she had to think for two people now. She was utterly and completely responsible for a new life. If the very worst happened, and Jacko found himself incapable of being a father, it was all on her.

It wouldn't happen, but she couldn't afford to not think of it, not with a child depending on her.

Okay. She faced her fears squarely. If worse came to worst, she could do this. She could raise a child on her own. She owned her home and she had part of her mother's estate. Her design business was booming. She lived in a crowd of people who would help her in any way they could.

The ASI crowd was not fair weather friends. Every single person had known tragedy and had shown themselves to be people you could count on for the long haul.

She'd be okay on her own. Jacko was coming back, but if somehow his demons were too big for him to face, she could do it, she could raise their child on her own.

Feeling more settled, she ate a croissant packed in the cooler—excellent, Isabel really was special—and had a cup of tea and went into her study.

She got absolutely nothing done that day.

John Huntington, founder of ASI, stopped by with his wife Suzanne—on their way to the Lloyd Center, though the Lloyd Center was in the opposite direction—to see if she needed anything.

She'd barely closed the door behind them when Jack Delvaux showed up with a case of beer, self-inviting the poker group to meet at her house that evening and by the way, if she needed anything done in the house, to draw up a list.

Then Joe showed up with another cooler of food for the poker game, and by that time, it was dusk and she had to start setting up the poker table.

Everyone had kept her so busy today she'd barely had time to think of Jacko.

The sky was dark gray and the poker guys and their ladies started arriving, couple by couple. Soon the house was filled with noise and laughter.

Lauren had popped into the bedroom to grab her iPad to show Summer something when her cell rang.

Jacko.

Lauren sat on the pretty nursing chair in her bedroom—in *their* bedroom—because her legs shook.

"Jacko?"

Silence.

She drew in a deep breath. "Poker night is at our house tonight," she said gently into the silence. "Metal, Joe and Jack. And Felicity, Isabel and Summer. Isabel sent Joe over this afternoon with enough food to keep a prepper family happy for a year. I think Joe is missing you the most. He's going to miss taking money off you and he's going to miss your grumpy face when you lose. Everyone else is a graceful loser, you know."

She could hear breathing over the line. He was there, but he couldn't speak. Her heart cracked just a little. She knew how terrible she felt. How lonely and unsettled. *Just imagine Jacko*, she thought. His feelings must be overwhelming if he couldn't even talk to her.

She settled into the chair, tucking her feet under her. Lowering her voice, as if he were in the room with her, right next to her, so close she could feel his body heat. The way they sat when they listened to music together or watched TV together.

"You know," she said, "I was thinking about the night we—we got together, for want of a better term. Do you remember? Yes, of course you do."

He'd told her once his life started that night.

Her heart beat just a little faster and she wiped her eyes.

That night was imprinted on her, as well.

She'd been on the run for two years from a psychopath. She'd settled happily in Portland, making friends almost against her will with Suzanne. Jacko had somehow attached himself to her, always somehow there. He never made a move, actively avoided touching her, but he was always there just the same.

That night, she had reason to believe her new identity had been compromised and she knew she had to run. One last night in Portland, in the life she loved, was all she could allow herself.

She was going to seduce Jacko and leave the next morning. One last night of heat and sex before hitting the cold, lonely road.

"All the time you were driving me home, I was scheming how to get you to kiss me. To take me to bed. I was mapping the whole thing in my head. I was thinking—invite you in for coffee or a drink. Sit down next to you on the couch, maybe brush your hand with mine." She wiped away a tear. "I wanted that so much. I wanted *you* so much. Just one night with you, to take away a good memory before I went on the run again."

Lauren could almost feel the intensity at the other end of the line. He was listening to her with everything in him.

"But—but I was also telling myself I didn't stand a chance. You had a rep, you know? Suzanne and Allegra talked about you all the time. The guys did too. Nobody knew what to be more impressed by—the number of women you'd had sex with or your shooting scores." She gave a little laugh, watery and sad.

Silence.

Where was he? He was on the road, but where? Where was his quest taking him?

"So, I was scared out of my mind you wouldn't want me. They said you were a real player and you liked your women young and sexy—biker chicks. And I knew I wasn't sexy at all."

Though as it turned out, she turned Jacko on—a lot.

"Do you remember how hard my hands shook when you walked me to my door? I was planning on seducing you but I couldn't figure out how. I was so scared you'd take a drink, just to be polite, then leave and go to a bar and pick some chick up. I was having a panic attack. I couldn't feel my hands. Remember? I fumbled the keys and couldn't open the door, so you had to take the key and open it for me."

And the next thing she knew, she was plastered against the wall and Jacko was kissing her senseless.

He'd been thinking about it, just as she had. It was the beginning of their love affair and it had changed her world and his, forever.

"Do you remember, Jacko? Darling?"

Silence.

Lauren wiped away another tear, then swiped her thumb across the screen and closed the connection, following the sounds of laughter to where the poker game had started and Joe Harris was winning hand after hand.

In the kitchen, Felicity, Isabel and Summer were unpacking another cooler of delicious food. Isabel had already put a platter of thinly sliced pot roast in the oven to keep warm. Summer and Felicity had pulled out her dining room table and set seven places.

Lauren's heart thumped hard when she saw the missing place. She knew Jacko would want to be here. He hated losing, which he did on a regular basis because apparently Joe had some special connection to the Poker Gods. But Jacko loved being around his buddies and the animus disappeared once the poker game stopped.

Don't be sad, she told herself.

Jacko wasn't here because he couldn't be. There was something in him that was forcing him on the road. But *she* was here.

This was her tribe. Her child—*their* child—would grow up surrounded by these good, strong people, who would stand by her no matter what.

Jacko was alone with his demons. She had her tribe around her. She plastered a smile on her face as she sent a silent prayer for the man she loved. That he would complete his quest and find his way back home.

CHAPTER FIVE

Jacko put his cell down on the tray in the dashboard and pulled out from the wayside stop. He'd popped into a diner for quick fuel and a caffeine drink, the kind of thing Lauren would never let him eat. He couldn't even remember what he'd eaten. It tasted like cardboard.

Nothing on the road could beat Isabel's cooking anyway—it was world class. Right now the people he loved most were at his house, having a good time. It was true that Joe was taking money off Metal and Jack, but as compensation they'd have a great dinner afterward. Share a few beers, a few laughs.

They were there with Lauren, looking after her.

That was *his* job. Looking after Lauren, making sure she was safe and happy—that was what he was supposed to be doing, instead of being on the road, a thousand miles from home, on some half-assed quest to—to what?

As Metal put it—the fuck was he doing?

Jacko rarely got tired but all of a sudden he was swamped with fatigue. Something more than physical tiredness, something that was dangerous on the road.

He'd been driving for ten hours straight and had another seven hours at least before he got to Rancho San Diego.

A blinking sign by the side of the road showed a motel with vacancies. Jacko swerved and ten minutes later he had the keys to a room. He was too wound up to sleep but at least he could rest his eyes for a few hours.

The room was disgusting. Maybe a year ago he wouldn't even have noticed. He was used to living rough as a kid and as a SEAL on mission. Being dry and on something softer than the ground was already better than many ops he'd been on.

But now, after living with Lauren, it was a form of punishment being in this room. The smell assaulted him as soon as he turned the key in the lock in the plywood door a blind man could have picked in under a minute.

There were NO SMOKING signs everywhere in the motel but someone had recently smoked in the room, leaving that nauseating smell of stale cigarette smoke. Layered on that was the smell of filthy carpet and dusty curtains.

The bed sagged visibly. The bathroom door was open. Inside was a cracked yellowed sink. He checked the bathroom out, pulling back the ancient shower curtain to see some pubes on the shower stall floor.

It was okay. This was punishment he deserved. This crappy place was right for someone who at this very moment could be sleeping beside the most beautiful woman in the world—a woman who loved him—on a lavishly comfortable bed that smelled clean and fresh.

Jacko didn't even take his boots off. He just lay down on the dirty bedspread, put his hands behind his head and stared at the ceiling, waiting for dawn.

Thinking of Lauren.

Lauren, so very soft. Lauren, whose pale skin was a magnet for his hands, for his eyes, for his mouth. Lauren, who loved him.

If she were here right now, he'd be touching her all over, feeling where her body was already starting to change. He'd felt that the night he arrived home, without understanding. Minute changes invisible to someone who hadn't made a study of every inch of Lauren's body his lifelong mission.

The face just a little fuller, breasts a touch larger, nipples a little darker, not that pale pink he loved but a deep rose color he loved even more.

He'd put his hand over her belly without realizing what lay beneath it. If he had, he'd have freaked even earlier.

Goddamn.

Before his eyes, Lauren started changing shape. She was smiling at him while her body transformed. The breasts grew even larger, her belly swelled, rippled. Something inside her, fighting to get out.

The skin of her belly moved, bulging in odd places. It became like a beach ball, the skin shiny and taut, growing and growing. Jacko couldn't believe that Lauren kept smiling at him while her body was undergoing such a massive transformation. Her belly grew monstrously huge. Something kept moving under the skin, undulating like a snake under water.

Jacko put his hands on her belly, as if to contain it. Under the skin of his palms, he could feel something inside, moving. Something kicked against his hand, hard, like something fighting to get out. He pressed harder, to keep it inside.

Lauren kept smiling at him but tears started running down her cheeks. He frowned, wiped his thumb across her cheek. Not tears. Blood.

Her breasts, too. The nipples were…bleeding, thin trickles of blood from the nipples running down the underside of her breasts. Under his hand, what was in her belly poked at him hard, something *sharp*.

Lauren, bleeding tears but still smiling at him, sighed heavily as if suddenly tired. Her belly was rippling. She pulled her knees up, spread her legs, and Jacko saw that there was a lake of blood under her. He glanced sharply at her face and saw how pale she was, the trickle of blood from her eyes very dark against her shockingly white skin.

"Lauren?" Her eyes turned to him but they were cloudy. She was having trouble focusing. "Lauren, honey? Look at me." Jack made his voice sharp, to catch her attention. He was never sharp with Lauren but she seemed to be moving further and further away from him, though she wasn't moving from the bed. Her eyes drifted shut. "Focus! Damn it, Lauren, *look at me!*"

She wasn't responding and oh God, the blood! Jacko needed to get up and find something to staunch the bleeding but he didn't dare leave her side. He picked up her hand, that pretty hand he loved to hold, but she didn't curl her fingers around his as she usually did. Her hand was slack in his.

She was slick with blood now and he was frantic. The bleeding between her legs was heavy and he pulled the top sheet off the bed to stuff between her legs when all of a sudden her belly bulged obscenely and something appeared from her vagina. A black head of hair. Her body was pushing it out though she was unconscious, head slumped back, bloody eyes closed.

Jacko was sweating, frantic, not knowing where to help her, how to help her. He needed to call someone but in the meantime she was giving birth, bleeding, unresponsive.

"Lauren, look at me, honey, don't close those beautiful eyes, I want to see them, I want to see you looking at me, Lauren, honey—*Lauren.*"

He kept up the litany, in a panic. He never panicked but the situation was barreling out of control. A head slithered out from between her legs, one shoulder, the other—coarse black hair, deformed features. Eyes alive, watching him.

As Jacko watched, the creature *pulled itself* out of Lauren's body with long, spindly arms, this freakishly disjointed *thing*, slithering out in a gush of blood, blood Lauren didn't have to spare. The thing cracked her open, thin black fingers tearing her apart from the inside.

Jacko heard the crackling sound of Lauren's pelvic bones breaking. The pain had to be horrible, but she was unconscious, pale face still, eyes unmoving behind their lids.

The thing finally clawed its way out of her ravaged body, blood spurting, the white splinters of broken bones visible. Jacko reached for it to kill it but it slithered out of his grasp.

The thing scampered to the edge of the bed, multi-jointed legs working like a spider's legs. It crouched there for a second, head cocked, watching as Jacko frantically tried to soak up the blood that was rushing from Lauren, shaking her, shouting her name. He lifted up her shoulders and her head lolled, as if she were…

No. *No!*

With a hateful cackle, the creature leaped from the bed, scuttling like a cockroach across the room, disappearing out the door. Jacko couldn't race after it because he held a motionless Lauren in his arms, blood pouring from her ravaged body.

"Lauren," he whispered. Sound barely made it out of his tight throat. He was strong but there was nothing he could do against the damage that her body had suffered. "Honey, come back to me."

She shuddered in his arms and he pulled her tightly against him, holding her, rocking her. She didn't embrace him, her arms lying slack at her sides, hands open on the blood-soaked sheets.

He had one hand against her back and felt a long breath leaving her body. No breath coming back in. He held her even more tightly, his own harsh breathing loud in the silent room. Panic filled his head, he couldn't hear, he couldn't see, he couldn't think.

Another small shudder, a rattling sound in her throat, and he could feel life slipping from her. One last sigh and she collapsed in his arms. Pulling back, Jacko stared at Lauren through tear-swollen eyes and all he could see was a beautiful corpse, ravaged beyond recognition.

"*No!*" he screamed. "No no no!"

Her blank eyes stared back at him accusingly. He hadn't been able to save her and now she was dead.

The creature across the room stopped and looked back over its misshapen shoulder, head cocked, studying him out of black, fathomless eyes. Crooked lips lifted over bloodstained teeth. "She's dead," it hissed.

No!

Jacko bolted up in a rush, shaking. He was breathing hard, panting, sweat pouring off him in rivers. His head swiveled, looking around the room. Empty. He looked at his hands. Empty. Not holding a dead Lauren.

He checked the bedsheets. Not covered in blood. There was no monster creature across the room staring at him, taunting him.

Lauren wasn't dead.

It took a long time for his body to recognize that. It was shaking and shivering, convinced he'd watched her die.

Finally, he sat up against the dusty headboard, more exhausted than when he'd arrived. Somehow he'd fallen asleep and had a nightmare. If that was what he could expect when he fell asleep— watching Lauren die, torn apart and bleeding—he'd stay awake the rest of his life.

There was nowhere to go with his horror and dread. He couldn't go back to Lauren this way, simply couldn't. He was a wreck, convinced his child would be a monster that ripped her apart. Even when he closed his eyes for more than a minute, he could see the creature slashing its way through her, a goblin from the bowels of hell. His goblin. His hell.

Jacko sat on the sad bed in the dirty motel room until the sky outside the smeared windows turned faintly lighter. He exited the motel room, got into his truck and turned south, hoping to find something that would let him sleep without dreaming of demons.

He reached San Diego mid-morning, turned east onto 94 and the road started climbing up into verdant hills.

At San Diego he barely thought of Coronado, which was weird. It was just the turnoff point, not the turning point of his life.

San Diego was where he joined the Navy, Coronado where he underwent SEAL training. The Navy and the SEALs had turned his life around. In a very real sense, his life began the day he walked into the Navy recruitment office. The most important place in his life had been San Diego.

Until Lauren. Until Portland.

The day he first saw Lauren—*that* was the day his real life began. The day he was no longer alone in the world. The SEALs gave him brotherhood, so did ASI. But nothing in his life had prepared him for what it meant to be a couple. To know he would be with Lauren till—as the saying went—death did them part.

To be loved.

Before Lauren, he'd have laughed if anyone said he'd fall in love, and now look at him.

No one had ever loved him before Lauren and he was running away from her, just when she needed him.

But God, the image of that goblin, tearing her up from the inside…

He rolled into Rancho San Diego. It was a pretty, upscale dormitory town, full of expensive shops, galleries and restaurants. Mayer's office was on Catalina Boulevard, which turned out to be one of the main thoroughfares. It was so devoid of traffic he was able to park right outside the lawyer's offices.

Jacko got out of his SUV slowly and stretched. He felt stiff and creaky, like an old man. Like he'd had a bad flu for a couple of decades. He hadn't slept beyond the time of the nightmare but that wasn't it. On one op in East Africa they'd gone for two weeks on an average of a couple of hours' sleep every twenty-four hours, and he'd still been going strong when the op ended. Now he was wiped out with worry and self-loathing and homesickness and terror. He was feeling all of them, all at once.

There it was, a four-story brick building, big potted plants outside a brass and glass entrance. Jacko pulled out his cell, called the lawyer. He had called from the road to say he'd be arriving Sunday and Mayer had promised he'd keep the office open.

Mayer answered immediately and told him to come right in.

Jacko was dirty, tired. His clothes were rumpled and he was smelling none too fresh after so many hours driving. He hadn't shaved either.

Jacko had no pretensions to elegance, didn't even want any. Off-duty, he dressed in jeans and tees that, though clean, were well worn. When he was on official ASI business, he usually wore turtleneck cotton sweaters and sports jackets and occasionally slacks instead of jeans. He made an effort for his bosses to be presentable. He'd even removed his facial piercings and in winter, long sleeves covered his tribal tats.

But right now he was presenting himself as a rumpled thug with two days of stubble.

Fuck it.

He walked into the building, found a big brass board with company names etched on it and saw that Mayer & McLean Law Office was on the third floor. He took the stairs two at a time, needing the physical exercise.

Inside, it was everything he imagined a law office should be. Prosperous and quiet as they sued the pants off people on behalf of their clients. Jacko avoided having any dealings with doctors and lawyers if possible.

A very blond woman in clothes Lauren would approve of lifted her eyes, then widened them when she saw him.

"Yes?" she said in a voice that was supposed to make him cringe.

He just stared her down. "Morton Jackman. Here to see Mr. Ernest Mayer."

"I'm sorry." She didn't check anything. He didn't fit the profile of a Mayer client. That was okay with Jacko. He was used to not fitting anyone's profile. "Mr. Mayer is fully booked up. Today and tomorrow."

Fuck that. "Check your boss's schedule. See if he made room for me."

"I'm sure that—" She clicked and her heavily mascaraed eyes widened. She looked back up at him. "I was—um—mistaken. You can go in, Mr. Jackman, first door on the right. I'll announce you."

A Mr. Jackman to see you, sir, he heard as he went through the polished teak door with Ernest Mayer, Esq on a brass plaque to the side of it.

The door didn't open when he got within three feet from it like the ASI doors did. It was a good office, it smelled of money, but it wasn't anything compared to his company.

What the fuck was he doing here when he could be back in Portland, working at the coolest company on earth, then going home to the most beautiful woman in the world? He stood before the door until he heard a click and a female voice coming from a small box by the side of the door, asked him to come in

Ernest Mayer Esquire's office was guarded by a dragon lady—a middle-aged woman with steel-gray hair and glasses with those chain thingies attached to the temples. She looked like trouble and Jacko braced himself—but she surprised him by smiling warmly. "Go right in, Mr. Jackman. Mr. Mayer is waiting for you." She pressed a button and a red light went on over the door to Mayer's office. "I'll make sure nobody disturbs you."

Jacko opened the door a little warily, unsure what to expect. The last thing he expected was a hug.

This tiny guy—a hobbit, really, only with shoes instead of hairy feet—was clutching Jacko's waist, head full of wiry gray hair buried in his chest.

Jacko froze, arms at his sides, afraid to make any kind of move. *What the fuck?*

The geezer pulled back, snatched his wireless eyeglasses off his face and wiped his eyes. His hand wasn't enough so he pulled out a blindingly white handkerchief as big as a sheet, wiped his eyes with that and honked into it.

"Mr. Jackman." Jacko wasn't tall but this guy had to tilt his head back to look him in the eyes. "Please forgive me, emotion got the better of me." He indicated a client chair. "Please, sir, sit down. This is an amazing pleasure."

Jacko barely kept himself from looking behind him to see who the geezer was referring to. He sat down, gingerly, prepared to get back up fast if Mayer had mistaken him for someone else.

The guy didn't speak, just beamed at him in silence.

Okay. Jacko would have to get the ball rolling. "Mr. Mayer," Jacko began.

"Oh!" The geezer jumped in his chair. "How remiss of me! May I offer you something? Coffee? Tea?"

"Coffee. Thank you. Black, no sugar."

"Indeed." He pressed a button. "Marsha, could you please bring a cup of coffee and my usual tea? Thank you."

He folded his hands in front of him and just stared at Jacko, big smile plastered on his face.

This was getting very weird. Jacko tried again. "Mr. Mayer—"

"Your grandfather would have been so proud of you," Mayer said quietly. Alarmingly, his eyes were wet again. "I checked your records, Mr. Jackman. You have a very distinguished service record, and I suspect there were many brave acts that weren't in the official records. A SEAL." He shook his head. "Amazing."

"Thank you, Mr. Mayer. Now the reason for my visit—"

"Lee had no idea of your existence," Mayer interrupted. "None. His daughter Sara ran away and he never heard from her again. Broke his heart.

Alice never recovered and died of a stroke five years later."

"I had no idea I had grandparents, either," Jacko said quietly.

"I did some checking," Mayer said. "You were in and out of foster homes, while Sara was in and out of rehab and in and out of prison. I want you to know that if your grandfather had had any inkling of your existence, he would never have let you stay one day in foster care. Unthinkable. You had it rough in your childhood."

Jacko nodded. Yeah, he'd had it rough. But it was a long time ago.

"But you turned into a fine man, a brave soldier. And from what I could see on the website of Alpha Security International, a very successful businessman. Notwithstanding a brutal childhood. Sara has a lot to answer for, besides breaking her parents' hearts."

"Had," Jacko said. "And I guess she paid for her addictions. Her life was short and miserable."

Mayer nodded. "Cut off from her own family and from her own son. I cannot imagine anything worse. Her parents loved her dearly but after running off, they never heard from her again. They had no idea if she was dead or alive. It broke them."

"I didn't know them, I didn't know they existed. But I'm sorry they went through all that pain."

"Well." Mayer looked down at his desk and drew in a deep breath. He looked up and smiled. "A lot of harm has been done, but that's over now." He pushed a set of keys across the wide expanse of polished desk to Jacko. "The red keys open the gate, the blue key opens the front door, the green key opens the back door and the garage."

Jacko hefted the set of keys in his hand. They were like artifacts of a bygone era. Perfectly normal keys for locks that could be picked in a second by a toddler. Security clearly wasn't a big priority for Lee Garrett. He felt safe in his world. Jacko hadn't ever felt safe. His house was as protected as high tech could make it.

"Keypad codes?" he asked the lawyer.

Mayer's eyes went blank. "I beg your pardon?"

"Any keypads to access the property? I'd need the codes."

"Ah." The frown lines eased up, leaving only the lines of old age. "No. No keypads, no codes. Everything you need to get into the Garret estate is right there in your hand. I don't think Lee ever even contemplated keypads."

Or any other form of security, apparently. "Okay." Jacko wanted to get going. To get to this place, get a feel for it, find out what he could as fast as he could and then get back to Lauren. "I'll get these keys back to you when I'm done."

Mayer smiled. "No, sir, you will not. The keys, the farmhouse, the land and everything on it is now officially yours." He leaned forward and suddenly he no longer looked like a kindly hobbit, he looked like the worldly man he was. "I'll tell you a secret, Mr. Jackman."

"Jacko," he said steadily.

"Jacko, then. I may have stretched the law a little. Lee's will was very clear. He left his entire estate to his daughter, Sara. I could have had her declared legally dead. God knows I wanted to. Wanted her dead, actually, may God have mercy on my soul. I hated her because she caused my best friends so much pain. But, the fact is I didn't have her declared dead because Lee didn't want that. As long as he lived, he hoped she'd come home and wouldn't hear of her being declared dead.

"And there's something else. I am a lawyer, Jacko, and as such, I am legally bound to the facts of any case that crosses my desk. But I had a feeling I can't explain that something—someone— was out there. That Lee would find justice, even if after death. I think I somehow felt that you would someday show up, and by God, you have. I will expedite all the paperwork and forward it to you. As fast as the law allows, I will make sure the property passes over into your name. Lee deserved that, and you deserve it. I'll forward the deed to you at your company or your private address, whichever you prefer."

His words were like arrows piercing his chest. Jacko had never once thought of anything good coming from his mother, and here he found himself with a property. Belonging to his grandfather.

His grandfather. His grandmother. The words sounded strange, like rocks in his mouth. These two people he'd never met, never even imagined could exist. People who looked nothing like him but people who might have loved him had they known he existed. Who knew?

The only person who had ever loved him was Lauren. That was a bedrock fact of his life. But maybe...

Maybe he would have been loved by his grandparents. Who the fuck knew?

Now he was itching with curiosity to see the place, a place tied to him by blood and, if the geezer across the table from him was right, tied to him by tears.

Jacko rose and Mayer rose with him. He reached out a tiny, soft hand and shook his with a surprisingly strong grip. "Mr. Jackman, it's been a pleasure. Stay at the ranch as long as you like, of course. The deed will arrive in a few days, but I can assure you that the property is yours, free and clear."

"Thank you, Mr. Mayer. I'll keep the keys then but if—when I come back, I will be sure to let you know." He'd come back with Lauren. With his pregnant love. To look at the property his grandfather had left him.

Such crazy notions. Pregnant lover—soon to be his wife. Wife. Kid. Grandfather. Grandmother. For someone who'd been alone all his life, he was accumulating connections like crazy.

The old guy's eyes were wet as he shook Jacko's hand. "I'd be very grateful if you could give me a ring when you come back, Mr. —Jacko. It would be an honor to invite you out to dinner. Lee Garrett was like a brother to me. Alice, your grandmother, was one of my wife's best friends. My wife was devastated when Alice died. So do please let me know."

"Sure." The geezer was moved and damned if Jacko wasn't moved too. He was looking at the lifelong friend of his grandfather. Mayer had loved Lee Garrett like a brother, he said. Which made him practically Jacko's uncle. Great uncle.

Shit, this family business hurt his head.

"I will definitely call you when I come back," he said seriously. And he would. He just knew Lauren would love the geezer, whose eyes were getting wet again. Jesus, he had to get out of here fast, his own eyes were burning. Shit.

Jacko got back in his truck and made his way to the ranch. His grandfather's ranch. God.

Mayer had given him elaborate instructions and he had GPS but in the end it was easy as anything. He just took the main road north out of town, went ten miles, turned left and there it was. The house was on a slight rise so he could see it from outside the gates—big, imposing, abandoned.

One key opened the gate. Amazing. Kindergartens nowadays were better protected. How could people not be security conscious? The whole area was like Trust Central. None of the houses along the road had security cameras. Some didn't even have gates. You could just walk up to the front door.

It baffled him.

He'd been security conscious his whole life. Even in childhood, with drunk ex-boyfriends trying to batter their way into the trailer he shared with his mother. All the neighbors in the trailer park had been dangerous and he'd learned early and well to keep the place as secure as he could.

Being a SEAL hadn't done much to convince him the world was a safe place, either.

Must be a whole different mindset to live with no security, he thought as he opened the front door with another simple key. So simple you could open the door by blowing on the lock the right way.

It meant Lee Garrett and his wife had felt themselves protected their whole lives. And who knew? Maybe they were. Maybe growing up in a place where everyone knew your name was its own form of protection.

Though Jacko himself would take motion sensors and security cams over that any day.

The house was dark inside, all the shutters closed, curtains drawn. Someone had cleaned the place thoroughly; there were no smells of something rotten. The place smelled of dust and closed rooms. He entered carefully, boots making no noise at all, just as he'd been trained. He felt unsettled, exactly as if he were entering a possible danger zone.

No danger, though. No danger, no life, no nothing. Dust and silence. Jacko went from room to room, opening the curtains and windows, letting in the bright sunlight, airing the place out.

He felt weird doing it, thinking he had no right, though actually, he did. He had every right. The place was his.

Wasn't that a kicker?

His.

Jacko had never owned property. Ever. He had a lot of money in the bank and followed Suzanne Huntington's investment advice religiously and his money just kept growing. Kept making him more.

He lived with Lauren in the house she'd bought with her inheritance. Lately, they'd been talking about buying a bigger house, moving closer to the area where Joe and Isabel and Jack and Summer lived. Metal and Felicity were thinking of moving to the same area. He'd put in his money, too, and they could afford to buy something really nice.

And now that a kid was on the way...

Jacko stumbled and looked down at his boots on the wide, flat hardwood floor. There was nothing to stumble over, except what was in his head. The notion of his kid.

Focus.

Okay.

Jacko started with a big sideboard that was shoulder height. They were called madias. Jacko knew that courtesy of Lauren, who seemed to have an encyclopedic knowledge of types of furniture and styles going back to the caveman era. It was going to be fun bringing her here. She'd know the name for everything.

He was in an enormous living room that took up almost the entire ground floor, so presumably the bedrooms were on the second floor. The huge room was broken up into sections by the furniture and it was pleasant to look at. You could easily imagine a family in it.

The madia's top was filled with silver-framed photographs. It was like reading a book. It even went left to right. These were private family photos, unlike the ones he had looked at on Felicity's monitor.

The first frame on the left was huge and embossed. Lee and Alice's wedding photo. Mid-sixties, judging from the clothes. Jacko reached into his jacket pocket and pulled out the printout of the wedding certificate Felicity had found. Lee Garrett and Alice Hopfer, wed in San Diego in October, 1963, a month before Kennedy was shot.

Jacko studied the photo, angling it so that the bright sunlight streaming in showed up every detail. Lee and Alice looked young and happy. Lee had on an ill-fitting suit, white shirt and bolo tie which must have been really dorky in those days. But Alice was looking up at him as if he were George Clooney and Brad Pitt combined. She had on a flowing white gown, a crown of white flowers around her head, and was holding a bouquet of white roses. There were a lot of photos of the wedding. Lee and Alice cutting the cake, feeding it to each other, dancing outdoors in a pretty garden surrounded by smiling people clapping.

If you could look past the weird clothes, it was really sweet. Jacko didn't know these people and now never would, but he knew that their marriage had lasted a lifetime, ended only by Alice's death. Lee mourned her until the day he died.

Exactly the kind of marriage he wanted with Lauren. Forever.

Moving right, he saw a pregnant Alice, and an Alice with a newborn in her arms, Lee looking down at the baby with a smile on his face. From then on, it was all Sara, all the time. From toddler to grade schooler to high schooler.

A visibly happy family.

And then the photos stopped. There were only two others, and only the parents were shown: one of a birthday and the other of what looked like an anniversary. Both Lee and Alice were shockingly aged, bent and unsmiling.

Okay. He'd just seen a happy family turn into a desperately unhappy family, almost overnight.

Try as he might, it was hard to identify with them. His life and theirs had had no points in common other than Sara, and that was not a happy connection. And though he looked really hard, Jacko could see no physical resemblance at all between himself and the Garretts. He knew he hadn't looked like his mother, either, but then his mother had always looked like shit for as long as he could remember.

Okay, moving on. First he did a tour of the house to get his bearings. Everything was neat and squared away, coated with six months of dust. It was a comfortable house, kept in good repair, though nothing was new or fancy. The kitchen and bathrooms were dated, though serviceable. Whoever was going to buy the house would have to remodel. Gut it and start over.

Like a flash storm, something rebelled inside him at the thought of someone else living in the house. He couldn't figure that out. What the fuck was wrong with him? What the fuck did he care? He was going to sell. What was he going to do with a freaking house in Rancho San Diego?

Feeling uneasy, like he was invading someone's privacy, Jacko went through Lee's desk and found that Lee was a man who liked order. Bills were paid promptly, checkbooks balanced, taxes paid. He gave generously to charity and had made loans to friends, which had been paid back. He was a sponsor of the local library and had donated a pediatric dialysis machine to the local hospital.

He'd been a canny businessman, disciplined and organized. Lee owned shares in three quietly prosperous businesses—a feed store, a camping equipment store and a country club. The businesses brought in about three hundred thou a year.

Jesus. He inherited that stuff. Mayer had made it clear that he was sole heir, so Jacko owned shares in those businesses now.

Fuck. Jacko was…yeah. He was a rich man. With his own job, he would have an income of over half a million a year and property worth a million dollars. That was rich by anyone's count.

But he didn't come here for the money, he came for intel. He had a sense of Lee and Alice Garrett. And now for the hard part.

It was late afternoon when he found the courage to walk up the oak staircase and into Sara Garrett's bedroom. His mother's bedroom.

He was a grown man. He'd been in combat. He was tough as nails. And yet he hesitated on the threshold of the room. He'd put everything to do with his mother behind him, in a locked box. He didn't want to open that box, ever, but now he had to. *Do the hard thing.* The Navy SEAL motto.

The Garretts had left their daughter's room exactly as it had been when she'd disappeared. Jacko could picture Alice dusting and cleaning a teenager's room, even though Sara would have been a grown woman. It must have been amazingly painful, not knowing whether Sara was alive or dead.

Neither, as it turned out. Sara had been alive in only the biological sense of the word. Any humanity in her had died long before her body.

He did a perimeter walk. It was a spacious bedroom, where a girl could sleep, study, read, listen to music, entertain her friends. The furniture must have been top of the line at the time. Once he'd walked around to get a general feel, it was time to dive into the contents of the room.

He sat down on the pretty, delicate chair of her desk and heard it creak. Sara had been a slender teenager and they wouldn't have thought to buy a desk chair that could bear the weight of a man as big as he was.

The idea of breaking that chair freaked him, so he hunkered on the floor with her diaries and school notebooks and read about his mother's life as a child and teenager.

Unlike her parents, Sara had been wayward and rebellious by nature. Jacko could read it in her notebooks. English and math notebooks that should have been full of homework assignments were full of photos cut out from gossip magazines. The Bee Gees and John Travolta and The Eagles. Then the Sex Pistols and Alice Cooper. Sara's school notes were disjointed, ungrammatical, incomplete. A clear case of undiagnosed ADD, which at that time had probably not been on anyone's radar. Her grades were just passing. School wasn't important to her. Boys and clothes and makeup and music were.

Then, when she was seventeen, she met an older guy and it all went to hell. Jackman. What little she wrote was disjointed, handwriting all over the place, words making no sense. She began taking drugs and wrote of her "little friends." She was mad at her parents all the time. One page was just *I HATE THEM* written over and over in shaky handwriting.

And then, the notebooks took a turn toward the crazy. *Fuck* and *shit* written over and over, underlined until the paper tore. A teacher gave her a failing grade and Sara drew her face with a bullet hole in the forehead. She was sure some girls in her class were stealing from her. One page was a chilling scenario of blowing up the school.

It turned Jacko's stomach.

The explosion of craziness began when she started going out with the new guy, RJ for Robert Jackman. But more than the guy, it was the drugs. Weed, uppers and downers led fast to blow and coke. The kind of drugs that would mess up a young mind for good, forever.

A couple of weeks of frenzy, where her life seemed to be made up of sex and drugs and then...nothing.

Sara was gone, leaving two brokenhearted parents behind.

It was late afternoon when Jacko read the last of the notebooks. The golden light of the setting sun lit up the room—which was pretty and orderly, in contrast to the ugly mess of Sara's mind just before she ran away.

It was so hard for him to imagine anyone throwing away the life she'd had because he knew firsthand the life she ended up with. The filthy trailer house, the succession of low-wage jobs until she couldn't hold any job at all. Constantly scrambling for money to feed her habit, willing to do anything to anyone just to get one more high. Sara Garrett had left such devastation behind her—the grieving Garretts, himself. He was lucky he'd escaped intact from the disaster that was Sara.

What a waste.

Jacko's heart swelled with pity for the Garretts and with contempt for his mother. She wasn't a worthy daughter, and she sure hadn't been a worthy mother. But at least he knew her craziness wasn't hereditary. It was born with her and died with her.

Jacko was free.

As darkness filled the house, he realized his business here was over. There was one more stop to make but it was to complete the circle. The low-level hum of anxiety that had plagued him all his life—the fear his blood was somehow tainted on both sides—was gone.

In this pretty room of a teenager who'd thrown her life away, Jacko was made whole and would go back to his Lauren a better man. The man she deserved.

As the sun slid beneath the horizon, he pulled out his cell and called Lauren.

"Hello?"

Lauren's soft voice froze him. He opened his mouth and his throat clicked. He couldn't say anything at all. *Goddamn*, he was over this shit, wasn't he? He had a lot to say to her. Things she had a right to know. So why the fuck couldn't he talk?

"I hope you're finding what you're looking for, darling." He could just picture Lauren, in one of her jewel-tone track suits she never ran in, but wore when she created. Like an art goddess ninja. Right about now, she'd be curled up on the couch with a cup of tea and a book. Soon, she'd move into the kitchen for dinner. If he was coming home, she'd cook a nice meal. When she was alone, she often just had something light—a slice of cheese and fruit with a glass of wine.

No wine tonight, though. Because she was pregnant.

For the first time, that thought didn't send off alarm bells in his head. Before, he hadn't known how to handle the hot, jagged emotions flooding him every time he thought about the baby. Now?

He breathed out.

Her voice turned amused. "I just want you to know you're going to get a lot of flak from Metal when you get back. And Jack and Joe, too. I told them you'd come back just as soon as you could, but they're sort of mad at you. They'll get over it. I made it clear *I'm* not mad at you. You're doing what you think you need to do, otherwise you'd be here with me. I believe that with all my heart."

Jacko clung to his cell, fingers clutching tightly. It was a miracle he didn't shatter the plastic and Gorilla Glass. He was listening hard to every word she said, and to what was underneath the words.

Love. Love for him was in her voice.

"So do what you have to do, my darling. And take care of yourself. Stay safe."

His breath whooshed out of his body. She must have heard.

"I remember the first time I said those words to you," she continued. Her voice was lower now, softer. "It was the first time you left for a business trip after we started living together. I'd bought you that big thick cashmere scarf, remember?"

God yes. It was in his vehicle.

"You always take such good care of me, Jacko. Always making sure I'm comfortable and safe. I wanted to do something for you, so I bought that scarf. This was before I realized you honestly don't feel the cold. I got it for you because you made me shiver every time you went out in the dead of winter with a tee shirt and a jeans jacket. I noticed you always put my scarf on before going out, even though it probably makes you sweat. I'm sure you snatch it off your neck the instant you drive around the corner."

Bingo. He hung his head and smiled, his first smile in two days. It was a beautiful scarf and hot as hell. He hated wearing it.

"So I wrapped that scarf around your neck and kissed you and told you to be careful, to take care of yourself, and you froze and your eyes grew wide, as if you'd never heard those words before. And I thought—maybe he hasn't. Maybe no one has really looked after Jacko, cared enough about him to say those words. Your teammates sure wouldn't tell you to be careful. You guys are such hardasses, I am absolutely certain Metal has never told you to be careful. Not once, in all the time you've known him."

Yeah. No one had ever told him to take care of himself. Since childhood Jacko had done a really good job of taking care of himself, and SEAL training just made him stronger.

But…the thousand ways she showed she cared for him blew him away. She watched his diet, fussed over him if she thought he was getting sick. Jacko never got sick, ever, but he'd contemplated faking a sneeze because man, being on the receiving end of all that care was amazing. It took her a long time to realize he didn't feel the cold and she was always buttoning up his jackets, trying to get him to wear a wool cap. The big scarf was just the one thing out of many.

He heard her sigh and then she continued. "So I guess all of this is my way of saying—take care of yourself. Wherever you are."

She closed the connection and Jacko sat in the room while the sun disappeared and the room grew dark. Holding his phone in his hand, unwilling to break this connection with Lauren.

Finally, it was time. He stood up, walked downstairs. He took one final long look at the row of family photos, studying each face. Lee. Alice. Sara. He could see no resemblance whatsoever to him in any of the faces, but he was tied by blood to them. Two good human beings, one train wreck. Two out of three.

Not bad. Better than some.

Take his buddy Joe, for example. Drunk mess of a father, mom who ran away when he was a kid, drunk grandparents on both sides. And look at him now. Decorated SEAL, successful member of ASI. Engaged to Isabel Delvaux, scion of America's top political family, though they were all dead now except for her brother Jack.

Peace was settling inside him in this quiet room. He'd come to find out where he came from and now he knew. He came from two good people. His mom—she'd fallen into drugs so young it had scrambled her brains. His dad? Who the fuck knew? What difference did it make at this point?

None.

The blood of two good people flowed in his veins; that was all he needed to know.

The weight of a lifetime of unspoken doubt lifted from his shoulders. Jacko cracked his neck, shook his hands. He felt light. Free.

Time to go. He'd come back here, with Lauren. They'd decide together what to do with this house, the land. Sell it, keep it. Whatever she wanted to do was fine with him. He was okay with all of it.

Who knew? Maybe they'd keep it. Vacation here. God knows a vacation spot away from Portland's rainy climate might be fun. They could all fly down for long weekends. The house was big enough for the whole crew.

There was one last thing to do, one last burden from the past. It would take him a little over twenty-four hours. He hadn't slept much last night and the smart thing to do would be to sleep here and take off tomorrow morning for Texas.

But Jacko wasn't tired. He felt fine. He felt revved, even. He didn't need to sleep. He wanted to get this over with, get the lingering shadows out from his life so he could go back to Lauren free of darkness.

He was more than willing to become the husband she needed. And he was beginning to suspect he could be the father his child deserved.

Just one last thing to do before going home.

He headed out.

CHAPTER SIX

Lauren walked back out into the living room. She'd gone into the bedroom to take the call when she saw it was from Jacko. No one else should be listening.

It was so sad that he still couldn't talk to her. It was hard to think of the huge emotions raging in his chest. Jacko wasn't frightened of anything. It was what all his teammates said when they talked of Jacko in battle. He was fearless.

Not when it came to their baby, though. That scared him.

Her heart pulsed in pain for the man she loved.

"Is dickwad coming back anytime soon?" a sour voice asked. Metal.

Felicity backhanded him on the chest. "Don't talk like that. He'll come back when he can."

"When he can?" Joe said hotly. "When he *can?* If I ever dump Isabel like that, I hope you guys go after my sorry ass. With a gun."

Metal and Joe were Jacko's best friends. Jacko had saved Metal's life twice and she'd heard the story a million times. From Metal, not Jacko. Jacko never spoke of his missions. He'd worked really hard with Joe in rehab after Joe had been blown up and nearly died. The doctors said Joe would never walk again but Metal and Jacko had dedicated countless hours to overseeing Joe's rehab and he was now whole and healthy.

And pissed.

"*Joe Harris!*" Isabel's voice was loud and crisp and Joe snapped to attention, like a private when a general walks into a room. Lauren could see the whites of his eyes. He looked spooked.

"Yeah, honey?" he said, his voice tentative.

Isabel walked right up into his face and poked him in the chest, hard, with a manicured fingertip. Isabel came from one of the finest families in America and had an instinctively classy way about her. Lauren had never seen her angry, and certainly never angry at Joe. Right now, though, her eyes were shooting sparks.

Joe looked scared.

He was a Navy SEAL. He'd been in countless firefights. He'd shown immense courage time after time and had a chest full of medals for bravery that were in a shadowbox, never to be publicly acknowledged, but they were there.

Right now he looked terrified of a slender woman who came up to his shoulder.

"Joe Harris, you take that back right this moment and you apologize to Lauren. I've heard the stories about how surly and difficult you were during rehab. And who the hell stuck by your side, day after day, soaking up your insults and anger? Who?"

Joe's jaw muscles clenched. "Jacko."

"Everyone said you were impossible and yet he stuck by you and worked with you to get you back on your feet. And right now Jacko needs your help and understanding, if that isn't too tough a concept for you to wrap your mind around. Because if there is one thing I know—we all know—it is that Jacko loves Lauren. He has *not* walked out on her and you know it. He is doing something that must be incredibly important for him and just as he showed you loyalty, you should show it right back."

Joe's head was hanging. "Yes, ma'am," he said to the floor.

"I think you owe Lauren an apology. I think you know perfectly well that Jacko has not abandoned her. Even saying it is awful."

He took it like a man. Lauren had to give him that much. He lifted his head and looked Lauren straight in the eyes. "Isabel is right. I'm ashamed of myself. Whatever it is Jacko is doing, it's because he feels he has to and that's good enough for me. Should have been good enough for me right from the start." He eyed Metal. "We both owe him—and you—an apology."

"Yeah." Metal was hanging his head. "I called him about a bazillion times to give him grief. I know better."

"I told you Jacko knew what he was doing," Felicity said, exasperated. "And I told you to leave him alone. Didn't I?"

Metal nodded soberly. "Yeah. You did." He too looked Lauren straight in the eye. "No excuses. We're shitheads."

Felicity jabbed her elbow into his chest. Metal was almost as muscle-bound as Jacko. He wouldn't feel any pain from Felicity's elbow, but he did shoot her a hangdog look.

"Idiots," he amended.

"Morons," Joe added.

Isabel looked at Lauren. "Does that satisfy you? Because they really did go over the top. Say the word and I won't cook for Joe for a week."

Joe's eyes widened in terror. Once you got used to Isabel's amazing cooking, being deprived for a week was no joke.

Lauren smiled sadly. "Apologies accepted, guys. I know you love Jacko, too. We have to trust him."

"And I suspect Joe wants him back because he misses beating the pants off him at poker," Metal added.

Lauren laughed and everyone relaxed. She knew that their anger was basically puzzlement. Jacko had never been anything but…himself. In his own way, he was as predictable as the sun rising every morning. He was lethal on the battlefield and utterly reliable at work and at home. If he said he was going to do something, he did it. No question. If he made an appointment, you could count on him being on time. If he wasn't where he said he was going to be, he was dead somewhere—that would be the only explanation.

This kind of behavior—just disappearing without a word—was so unusual, it probably scared them. They thought they knew Jacko through and through, and he had turned into a puzzle they couldn't solve.

Lauren understood him better. She alone knew that he was sometimes chased by demons who visited him in the night. She'd wake up and he'd be gone from the bed, pacing the living room floor. Finally she'd pried out of him that he suffered from nightmares. They scared him, she could tell. He never said it outright but the unscareable Jacko was scared. As a man, Jacko was invincible, so the things he was scared of must stem from his childhood.

Jacko wasn't quite the monolith everyone assumed he was. He had cracks, just like every other human being.

She didn't care. The cracks, the nightmares, the demons didn't scare her. At the bedrock of his existence she knew he loved her, and she loved him.

Isabel clapped her hands. "Okay, now that I have officially forgiven Joe—and Metal—for being asses, I can announce that I made extra-strength dark chocolate brownies. Guaranteed to put hair on your chests, and that includes you, Felicity and Lauren. Let's eat."

As Lauren went into the kitchen to get plates and glasses, she paused for a moment, hand over her belly, right over where their child rested.

I hope you're okay, my darling. Come back to us soon.

Jacko drove through the night again, not feeling the fatigue at all. If anything, he felt energized, like someone clearing out old brush to build a new house. Getting rid of the old to make way for the new.

It was noon by the time he pulled into Cross, Texas. He looked around curiously at the town he hadn't been back to since leaving at seventeen. He'd never expected to come back, ever, but here he was.

Life was funny that way.

Cross was basically an intersection, and it was even more forlorn than it had been when he had left. It had three stoplights now instead of four. *Welcome to Cross, Texas, Population 2,378* the sign said. A whopping 1,000 fewer people than when he'd left. There'd been the ruins of a shopping mall about five miles out of town. But the businesses were closed and the parking lot empty. Main was pretty empty too. Just another dusty Texas town with no oil and no high tech, an economy based on failing ranches and stores that sold only the basics . You wanted fancy food, fancy clothes, books, you drove a hundred miles to Werring.

Jacko knew exactly where to go. It had been a long time, sure, but the sheriff's office wouldn't have moved. Nowhere for it to move to. Jacko rounded a corner just off Main and there it was. *Wyatt County Sheriff's Office.*

Jacko knew the inside of that office intimately. Not because he got in trouble with the law—he'd had two scrapes and then had gone off to the Navy. No, he'd been in and out because of his mom. She'd been incarcerated a lot of times, until Sheriff Pendleton had grown sick of locking her up. Jacko had always been there to take her back home once she'd dried out or sobered up.

Pendleton had been the closest thing he'd had to a friend then. Gruff, no-nonsense, he'd kept an eye out for Jacko. His wife Leanne often sent leftovers, the only cooked meals Jacko had until he'd taught himself the basics of cooking. Pendleton also left packages of used clothes on the trailer stoop. Clean, serviceable stuff that Jacko wore until they fell apart. They were his only source of clothes until he was old enough to do odd jobs.

Jacko remembered like yesterday his last talk with Pendleton, a former Marine. Pendleton had pressed a card into his hand the night he'd landed in the emergency ward after his mom's dealer had cut him up for trying to stop her from buying more drugs.

"Things aren't going to get any better, son," Pendleton had said to him, dark eyes sad. "Here's the card of a Marine buddy of mine. Join the Marines. You're better than this, and you *deserve* better than this. There's nothing for you here. Get out and never come back."

And that's exactly what Jacko had done, only he'd gone into the Navy not the Marines. It had been a toss-up between the Navy and the Corps. He knew he'd have made a good Force Recon sniper, but the Navy and the possibility of becoming a SEAL had won out. He'd taken Pendleton's advice and never gone back. The instant he'd left Cross, his real life had begun.

Pendleton had never expected to see him again, he knew that. But...he owed the man. One last debt. He'd pay it and he'd be gone again forever, the past cleared. Pendleton would be retired by now, but the current sheriff would know where he was. If Pendleton had died, Jacko would visit his gravesite.

Jacko parked next to the beaten-up Cherokee with *Wyatt County Sheriff's Office* painted on the sides. Looked like Wyatt County hadn't come up in the world.

Inside, the smell was the same—industrial cleaner and burned coffee. The place had always been shabby but Pendleton had made sure that everything was clean and in good repair. It now reeked of neglect. Old-fashioned phones with rotary dials that looked like they weighed ten pounds each, grimy old-fashioned computers with deep monitors, encrusted keyboards and ancient processors.

You'd think there'd be some federal money coming in. Back in the day, Cross had been smack in the middle of drug smuggling routes and there'd been a three-way drug war between two Mexican gangs and an Anglo-Mexican gang. When Jacko was twelve, two headless bodies had shown up in the middle of Main, the underground cartel wars bubbling up to the surface.

As a SEAL, Jacko had been briefed for a mission into Colombia—the rescue of a fallen DEA agent. The planners of the mission had showed him maps of the drug wars flowing back and forth across the border. Several times, the flow of drugs and money and arms and murders swept over Cross, though on some maps it was too small to show up.

A secretary looked up when he walked in the door, ancient, looking like she'd been there since the Carter Administration. She'd been staring at her monitor. From where he stood, Jacko could read *E! Entertainment* at the top of the screen. She stared at him, cocking her head, unimpressed.

"Heyup yeew?" she said in pure Texan. He'd forgotten how many vowels people could put into short words.

He leaned an elbow on the counter. "Yeah. I'd like to see Sheriff—the sheriff, please."

Damn. He'd forgotten to look up the guy's name. He should have pulled over and checked—would have taken him all of two minutes.

She wrinkled her brow, like the words "see" and "sheriff" were new to her.

"Got an appointment?" she asked finally.

If this had been a business thing, Jacko would have had an appointment fixed at least a week ago, and the printout of the confirming email with him. Fuck. Either he was losing his touch or he was really out of it. Maybe both.

"No," he said. Pointless trying on a charming smile. Jacko had no charm. And he couldn't shoot his way inside, either. Shit. "I don't."

The girl pursed her lips. "Sorry," she said, not looking sorry at all. "The sheriff is—"

"Candy." She turned to the big tall guy who'd just come out of a side door. "I'm in." The man held out his hand to Jacko. "Sheriff Constable. And

129

yes, I know constable means police officer in England. What can I do for you, Mr.—"

"Jackman," Jacko said. The handshake was dry and not a grip-strength contest. Jacko would have won. His grip had been measured by dynamometer at 60 kg—enough to crush bone if he wanted. He didn't want to crush this guy's hand. All he wanted was some intel before he got out and never came back. "If I can speak with you for a moment... I won't take much of your time."

"Sure. Step into my office," Sheriff Constable said with an affable smile, which faltered as he looked at Jacko's face. The sheriff was frowning, which made Jacko wonder what the fuck was on his face. Jacko should be smiling back. Right? He'd been told his default expression was ferocious with an overlay of dangerous. Lauren's words. He was about to ask for a favor from this guy. He should be smiling, too. He lifted the corners of his mouth. That should do it.

But for a long moment, the sheriff just stared at him. Then he seemed to shake himself and opened the door to his office.

The sheriff's office was big, but the walls needed painting and there was the same low level of technology. A glory wall to the right, framed photographs of Constable with men who were supposed to impress the onlooker. Jacko didn't recognize too many. A governor here, a senator there. A Fortune 500 CEO. The rest were self-important faces Jacko didn't give a shit about.

On another wall were a couple of antique guns mounted on boards behind glass and a small bookcase with legal texts. The third wall had wanted posters—not only of men wanted by the state of Texas but also the FBI's Most Wanted.

Constable sat down behind his desk and motioned Jacko to sit in the visitor's chair. Constable leaned back in his swivel chair, hands linked behind his neck. Body language as relaxed as it gets.

"So, Mr. Jackman, what brings you to Cross?"

Jacko kept an even voice. "I lived here from 1980, when I was born, until 1997, when I joined the Navy. I was friends with the sheriff then, Kurt Pendleton."

Constable's hands unlinked and he straightened in his chair.

Jacko frowned. "What? Is he—is he dead?"

As a kid, Pendleton had seemed ancient to Jacko, but he must have only been in his forties, which would make him about seventy now. Not that old, nowadays. But cops led dangerous lives. Not as dangerous as soldiers, but almost. In general, cops lived about twenty years less than civilians.

"No, sir. Pendleton isn't dead, though some might question that. He's in a home." Constable sighed, tapped his temple. "Not quite…right. Up here. He was making big mistakes, forgetting things. The city council relieved him and gave the job to my predecessor, who retired five years ago. Pendleton is in a special care home near Las Vegas. His son made the arrangements, or so I heard. I never met the man myself. Sorry."

Okay. Las Vegas. It was doable, on his way back to Portland. It would probably be sad to see Chief Pendleton now, a broken-down old man missing a few dots from his dice. But Pendleton had been good to Jacko back in the day. Maybe Jacko could leave some money with his caregivers, ease the old guy's life. Jacko was on a quest to wrestle his past to the ground. Seeing the old sheriff was part of that, he could feel it.

Jacko stood. "I appreciate your help, sir. Do you happen to know the name of that home where Sheriff Pendleton is now?"

The Sheriff frowned. "I don't, actually. But I can try to find out. If you'll wait here, I'll do my best to get an address for you." He walked out of his office before Jacko could say anything.

Jacko sat in the sheriff's office and waited. There were no sounds from the outside world, Cross as dead now as it had been when he was a kid. About the only thing Cross had was sunshine. A shaft of sunlight so strong it looked like it could bear weight shone through a none-too-clean window pane and created a bright rectangle on the linoleum flooring.

He checked the weather in Portland on his cell. Rainy, high of 45 degrees. Cold weather never bothered him, but it did Lauren. She loved sunshine. He'd take her with him when he returned to Rancho San Diego to look at the house. She'd soak up the sunshine and they'd decide together what to do. Sell, keep. He didn't care. Whatever made Lauren happy.

Maybe they'd toggle over to San Diego and he'd book them into the Del for a few days—the beautiful, old turn-of-the-last-century hotel on Coronado. Right on the beach. She'd love that.

It was an expensive hotel, old-fashioned luxury. When he was a SEAL, training in Coronado, the idea of staying at the Del was about as plausible as a vacation on the moon. One night cost a week's wages and at the time, Jacko had no savings.

Now, he could probably live at the Del, if he really wanted to. If he didn't order too much room service.

Man, his life had changed since those days. For the better. And he had Lauren.

Ferocious desire to be back with her exploded in his chest. It felt like scissors and knives—sharp, painful. If he could push a button to get back to her *right now* he would. He'd push that button and leave Cross, Texas, and beam himself straight back to her.

Whatever he thought he'd learn, he'd learned. He was done here. He'd never find out who his father was. That tiny hope that had been at the back of his mind forever was gone.

Sometimes Jacko had had this weird feeling that Pendleton knew who his old man was. Jacko had nothing to base that feeling on, really. Just an odd look and a word or two. But Pendleton had never come out with it, and now, even if he'd known, he probably couldn't remember. Jacko had never pressed it. If Pendleton didn't want to tell him, it was probably bad news.

There was just no way to track his dad down and it was probably better that way. Who knew who he was? Some druggie asshole drifter who'd passed through town at a moment when his mom could barely remember to eat let alone take care of birth control. She'd had her tubes tied after giving birth to him.

At least part of his heritage wasn't druggie asshole, if you didn't count his mom. Which he didn't. Her getting hooked was because she'd had undiagnosed ADD and his grandparents had been too naïve to recognize the signs. So she'd fallen into the ugly black hole of addiction, a place too horrible for life, like an airless, sunless planet.

But her side of the family was *normal*. His kid wasn't going to be born with two heads and fangs. And of course there was Lauren, who was perfect, and was giving their baby her genes, too.

Their baby. Jesus, he was having a *kid*. It finally settled inside him, the full weight of this. He'd been too freaked to grasp it, hold it, look at it. He did so now, this idea that had been too hot to handle, too fucking scary to deal with.

A baby.

A tiny little defenseless creature who would depend on them for everything. And they'd do it. Fuck yeah. He and Lauren would do it. They'd take this little thing and love it and protect it and watch it grow into a strong adult, and they'd be with the kid every step of the way.

Lauren's parents hadn't been too hot either. Her father had been weak and had dilapidated the family money before kicking the bucket and her mom had then married a Florida mobster. Lauren hadn't been loved and protected—though there'd been plenty of money—and she'd done okay. Lauren was the finest woman he'd ever met and ASI was lousy with fine women. Neither he nor Lauren had had good parenting and they'd turned out all right. In Lauren's case, more than all right.

So they could do this.

Yeah. Oh yeah.

Get back to Lauren, Jacko thought, the fastest route possible. The digging was over. He'd found out some good things, and he was ready to go back home. He'd get some flak from Metal and Joe and Jack, and his bosses would look at him squint-eyed, the way they'd done in the military when you didn't complete your run in the allotted time. Of course, in civilian life they couldn't command him to drop to the grinder and pump out 150.

They'd find a way to make him pay. Overtime, maybe. That was fine. Jacko knew there would be a price. Nothing came free. He could do overtime, no question.

So where the fuck was the sheriff? Jacko didn't need him. Felicity could run Pendleton down in under a minute. He'd give the sheriff another five minutes, then he was gone and the hell with him.

But the sheriff came back in two minutes, shaking his head, looking sorry. "Mr. Jackman," he said, walking through the door into his office. "I do apologize. I can't find anyone who knows where Pendleton's rest home is. Maybe if you wouldn't mind staying till after lunch, I can ask Charlie when she comes in for the afternoon shift. She's not answering her cell."

He was frowning.

"No problem," Jacko said easily, rising. It was all suddenly too much. Wasting time in this dusty office in a backwater town where he'd been miserably unhappy. There was nothing for him here and he was sorry he'd come. He couldn't wait to escape, to get back to Lauren. "But I need to get going."

The sheriff cocked his head. "Say, you never did say where you live now. If you have a card on you, I'll call when I get the name of the facility. Be a pleasure to do my predecessor a solid."

"I'm out of business cards," Jacko lied. He didn't want to leave any ties behind. He was done with Cross and would never come back. He'd find out what he needed to know his own way. "So, thanks for your help." He stuck out his hand.

"Sorry to see you go." The sheriff took it almost reluctantly. "Didn't even get a chance to offer coffee. Ours isn't bad. Crew took up a collection and we got ourselves a fancy coffeemaker."

"Another time." *Meaning never.* Jacko gave a brief smile and walked out the door. He paused on the steps leaving the sheriff's office and looked up and down the street. Some of the buildings he remembered from the bad old days, some were new but already in disrepair. Nothing here held any good memories for him. This was a place from a long-ago past that had nothing to do with him now.

He made his way down the steps, got into his SUV and headed north, happy to be leaving Cross behind him forever.

Fuck!

Stu Constable opened up his desk drawer and pulled out an old photo. It had been handed to him by his predecessor and Constable had been holding on to it for close to ten years.

Five hundred grand. He was looking at a face that represented five hundred grand. Five hundred thousand dollars was enough to pay his debts, get him out of this shithole and provide a stake in a new business.

He stared at the photo of the man in the photo. Tough-looking guy, cold eyes. He had long graying sideburns and a full head of dark hair. Wearing an '80s-style shirt with long pointy collars. But none of that was important. What *was* important was that he looked exactly like the man who'd just been in Constable's office.

The man in the photo had darker skin but that might be an effect of a photo that was over thirty years old. He also had pale eyes. Constable couldn't tell if the eyes were pale blue or gray. He had hair and the guy who'd just left had a shaved head. Other than that, he looked exactly like the man who'd just been in his office, Jackman. The resemblance was uncanny.

He punched in a number.

"*Si?*" A male Hispanic voice.

"Hey," Constable said. Good, the number was still valid. "This is Stuart Constable in Cross, Texas. That guy you want, Dante Jimenez? You still want him, don't you?"

He started sweating. A lot was riding on this. Five hundred thousand dollars would turn his life right around. Maybe convince his wife to stay with him. She was sick of being a sheriff's wife in a dump of a town. 500K would be a stake in a new life. He could buy half his brother-in-law's thriving diving equipment business in Galveston. Get out of this place, finally. Fuck the half-assed cop pension.

"Yeah," the guttural voice answered. "We still want him. Price has gone down, though. Two hundred grand."

Constable slumped in his chair. *Fuck!* He waited a second to make sure his voice was cool and calm. Two hundred grand was still a lot of money.

"I think I have a lead."

"You *think* you have a lead?" the voice asked sharply.

Shit! He couldn't lose this!

"No, no! I have a lead. A good one." Constable wiped his brow with the back of his hand.

"Stay at this number," the voice said and disconnected.

Constable listened to empty air then thumbed his cell off. *Stay at this number.* For how long, dammit?

He heaved a sigh. Pointless fooling himself. He'd sit in this fucking broken down chair until he starved and cobwebs covered his body. And it wasn't like he had something else to do. Cross was dead, day and night. Even the faintest possibility of making some real money—that was enough to keep him where he was.

An hour later, his cell rang. *Unknown number.* Okay. Maybe his request was making its way up through the ranks. Maybe he was going to talk to Gustavo Villalongo himself. No, wait. He'd died in prison years back.

"Talk." A different voice. Coarse and raspy. A smoker's voice.

"I have a photo to send. I'll need an email."

"A *photo?* What the fuck am I going to do with a photo?"

Sweat broke out across Constable's forehead. "You'll understand when you see it. But I need half the money before I send it."

Silence. "Do you know who this is?"

"Ah—" Now sweat was trickling down his back. "Ca-Carlos Villalongo." The heir to the Villalongo cartel. It had been the most powerful cartel along the Mexican border, operating both in the States and in Mexico. Until a DEA undercover agent had risen through the ranks to become Gustavo Villalongo's right-hand man and then smashed the cartel. The old man had been sent to American prison. The Villalongo cartel never recovered and Carlos proved to be a weak leader. But cruel, crueler even than Los Zetas south of the border.

His hatred of the DEA agent who'd put his father in prison was legendary.

Constable gathered his courage. This was his one shot out of his life. Another would never come his way again. "Send me half the money and I will send a photo. If you're interested, then I'll tell you how to track the man in that photo."

"Do you know what will happen to you if you are tricking me?" Carlos Villalongo asked, his voice full of quiet menace.

A minor skirmish with a rising cartel near Laredo had finished with a series of heads on pikes lining a country road. The entire leadership of the cartel. And their women and children lay in a pit, bullets to the backs of their heads having put an end to their misery.

Constable swallowed, tried to steady his voice. "I understand full well. But you will not be disappointed."

"Bueno. Write down this address." He dictated a Gmail address. "I will wire the money. Stay at this number."

Both of them knew that was the only money Constable would see. But that was okay. If he got paid the full price, and for some reason the tracker he'd put on Jackman's vehicle came loose and they lost him or they were unable to take this Jackman guy down —and he looked really tough and perfectly capable of handling himself—then they'd come back to him and take their frustrations out on his hide.

The tracker on the vehicle was the only thing Constable could give. His fucking video cameras didn't work. Hadn't worked in years and the county was too cheap to replace them. Luckily, he'd gotten his secretary to take photos with her cell phone of Jackman's face as he was getting into his vehicle. He tracked down the vehicle tags. They were Oregon license plates but were registered to some company headquartered in Delaware. So God only knew where that SUV was going.

If he only got half the reward money and they botched the grab and snatch, they'd consider it a fair deal. At least they wouldn't come after him to dismember him and scatter his parts all over the county.

So okay.

"Now give me your bank info."

Constable gave it to him.

God. Fifteen years ago, when the sheriff who had taken over from Pendleton handed him the keys of the sheriff's office and told him about how Gustavo Villalongo had been taken down by a DEA special agent, he'd also told him how Villalongo had a reward on the agent's head. A big one.

"Write down this number," the sheriff had told Constable, "memorize it, then burn it. And get yourself a bank account outta the country. In one a' them tax havens, where no one can get to your money. Because if you come across any info about where that agent went to, you're gonna rake it in. Man, Villalongo's got a hard-on for this guy, and he'll have it till he goes to his grave."

So Constable had memorized the number, burned the piece of paper and opened an account in the Caymans. Hadn't been easy, no sir. Rich guys did it all the time but for someone like him, he'd had to travel there and deposit five thousand dollars, just to open a fucking account. It burned him, but now look. He was ready. The brass ring had fallen right into his hands.

The old sheriff had made him promise he'd get a percentage of the take if he cashed in, but Constable reckoned he'd keep the whole thing. No reason to share.

In the movies, bank transfers were instant. On the screen was the bank account, a big line arcing over to it, numbers rolling. Insta-money.

Nope. The freaking thing had been inactive so long, when he finally found his password he discovered it'd been deactivated. So he tried online and finally had to call the frigging bank. And got frigging voice mail.

When he finally saw his bank statement he just stared at the numbers. One hundred grand. Plus the five grand he'd deposited years ago.

Five minutes later he sent the tracking coordinates.

Laredo, Texas

Carlos Villalongo picked up the photograph that had been emailed to him, together with coordinates from the tracker that idiot sheriff had put on the guy's vehicle.

Dante Jimenez. Only not. Younger than Dante. So—Dante's son, under the cover name of Jackman. Get the son, get the father.

Dante Jimenez. The name was enough to send his blood pressure soaring. Jimenez had posed as a drifter with a taste for violence and a deep knowledge of weaponry called Juan Diaz. He'd been perfect. Jimenez had pushed his way up through the ranks through intelligence and ruthlessness until he'd been his father's right-hand man. His father had defeated the Guadalajara cartel and was busy sweeping up the smaller gangs, consolidating them, making them part of his efficient system. In 1979 he'd taken in a billion and a half dollars, at the time a fortune so large it rivaled the big family fortunes of the east coast.

Gustavo was starting the move to distance himself from the day-to-day operations, leaving everything in the capable hands of Diaz/Jimenez, starting to plan his son's college education—Harvard or Yale, and he was perfectly prepared to make a huge donation to ensure his son's acceptance—when it all blew up in his face.

Because the man he knew as Juan Diaz, the man he'd considered his natural heir, was a famous undercover agent, a legend in the DEA. And the man who'd engineered the cartel's downfall.

His money confiscated, tried as a US citizen and condemned to forty years in a maximum-security federal prison, Gustavo's fall was complete. Carlos didn't go to Harvard and didn't go to Yale. He barely finished high school and he'd spent his adult life trying to piece together the remnants of his father's empire.

But even from prison, Gustavo had made sure Jimenez paid a heavy price. He had two of Jimenez's cousins shot dead and he'd targeted a woman Jimenez cared about. After which Jimenez disappeared from view, though he was still hunting them. Jimenez knew all the Villalongo secrets.

So Gustavo put out a big reward for news leading to Jimenez's whereabouts because he wouldn't rest until he had Jimenez's head. Sent to the Washingtom office of the DEA in a bag.

But Jimenez disappeared, and not all of Gustavo's dwindling resources could bribe, extort, or beat the name out of anyone. Gustavo's heart had exploded in his chest in prison from rage and confinement. Carlos had barely survived the attack on his cartel upon his father's death.

What should have been one of the great, historic cartels, more powerful than governments and almost more powerful than God, sputtered and almost died.

But now, he had leverage over Jimenez.

Find the son, find the father.

CHAPTER SEVEN

Green Orchards Rest Home
Henderson, Nevada

The rest home was just outside Henderson, Nevada, a suburb of Las Vegas. Felicity found it in the time it took him to get behind the wheel of his SUV, bless her. It was called *Green Orchards*, and it specialized in caring for sufferers of Alzheimer's and vascular dementia.

Jacko shuddered as he put his truck into gear. God. One of his worst nightmares, losing his marbles. All through his childhood, with no support, no family to speak of, nothing to his name, at least he'd always had his brains, and it had been enough. He'd pulled through, done well by himself.

All you really needed was right between your ears.

Once you lost that, you lost everything.

By the time Jacko was on the road that would take him to Las Vegas, Felicity had sent him all of Pendleton's info. When he'd been admitted, his clinical diagnosis, a list of the physicians and nurses who dealt with him, mini-mental tests administered over the years.

According to the files Felicity had, Pendleton's dementia was slight, stage two, which was one of minor memory impairment. According to Felicity, who'd done some background digging as only she could do, it was Pendleton's son who'd had him admitted to the special care facility.

Jacko could read between the lines. Old Pops was getting forgetful, had been pushed into retirement, the obvious thing was moving in with Junior or at least close enough for Junior to look after Pops.

But Junior—in the person of Tom Pendleton, Esq, with a thriving law practice in Connecticut— had no desire to be a caregiver and had rushed Pops into a well-known facility, which cost Pops his entire pension and big chunks from the sale of his house.

Jacko pulled over and, out of curiosity, opened the file Felicity had put together on Tom Pendleton. Christ, Jacko hated him on sight. Tall, thin, a thousand-dollar haircut and a five thousand-dollar suit. Partner in a big law firm. Tenth largest law firm in the country.

No, Tom Pendleton wouldn't have time for a father who needed a little help.

Jacko sighed. That had been his knowledge of the world before Lauren. Dog eat dog. Look out for yourself because no one else is going to. Lauren had taught him about love, had taught him that no sacrifice was too big for someone you love.

He got it.

Till death do us part.

When they got married, when he said those words to her, it would be heartfelt, meant with every fiber of his being.

Tom Pendleton lived in another world, a different one from the one Jacko now inhabited, where commitments were total and lifelong.

He wanted to call Lauren but…he was done with phones. Henderson would be his last stop on this trip down memory lane. Soon he'd be on his way home and he wouldn't have to listen to Lauren's voice over the airwaves, he could listen to her voice directly. Holding her tight, never letting her go.

For the first time since leaving Portland, Jacko could breathe. That band of barbed wire wound so tightly around his chest was gone. He was on his way home. One stop and then he was heading straight back to Portland, to Lauren, to his child. To his job, to his buddies, to his *life*.

It was late afternoon when he stopped just outside Henderson. He was traveling west and the sun was shining directly into his eyes.

He hadn't heard Lauren's voice today. He missed it. He missed *her*. He told himself he was done with phones, but that was bullshit. Even Lauren's voice over his cell was better than nothing.

Maybe he could talk to her now, finally. That huge boulder in his throat that had stopped him from talking to her was gone. But at this point, there was so much to say and he wanted to say it with her wrapped in his arms. Once he finished here, it was about a fifteen-hour drive back up to Portland, if he wanted to respect speed limits. No use getting pulled over and hassled. Fifteen hours was a long time, if you counted how much he missed her. But nothing compared to the rest of their lives.

Get this over with, put it behind you and go home.

The GPS brought him right to the sloping lawn of Green Orchards, a little oasis in the surrounding desert. There was minimal security at the gate. Jacko leaned out, pressed a button and a disembodied voice asked him his business.

"Visitor for Kurt Pendleton," he said, fully prepared to show documents. But nothing was necessary. He was buzzed in.

There was easy access to the patients, too. It was a weird feeling for him. Jacko had security tattooed on his brain. It was a vital part of him, like his hands and feet. He frowned at the lack of security. But…there was staff everywhere and a lot of the patients had visitors. From the happy glow on many wrinkled faces, the visitors were very welcome. So maybe making a visitor to someone in a home jump through security hoops every time they came would make for fewer visitors.

Huh. Security as a bad thing. That was really hard for him to wrap his head around.

Pendleton was in room 212, Jacko found out by asking the nurse at the desk. The nurse also told him Mr. Pendleton moved in and out of focus, like a shortwave radio. She used longer words, but that was the gist of it. His hold on reality could at times be "delicate" and "sporadic".

Ah, Kurt, Jacko thought sadly as he walked down the corridor. The Pendleton he knew had been sharp and present in the moment, and had had eyes in the back of his head. Back in the day, there wasn't anything happening in Cross, Texas that Pendleton didn't know about.

Room 212. The door was ajar and Jacko nudged it open with his knuckle. Pure habit, not leaving fingerprints. The room was nice, the last rays of sun shining in on a slant. A man was sitting in a chair with his back to the door, looking out the window.

At the sound of the door opening, the man turned around.

Kurt Pendleton. Jacko would have recognized him anywhere. He hadn't aged much. Jacko suspected that when he was younger, he looked older than he was, simply because he took on so much responsibility. And now he looked younger than his years, maybe because all of that responsibility was gone.

Pendleton stood and looked at Jacko, puzzled. Frowning, as if seeing him from a thousand yards. Then his face cleared and joy lit it up.

Jacko wasn't a smiling kind of guy, but he could feel a smile coming on. After all these years, Jacko was talking to someone who'd known him when he was a youngster. Everyone Jacko knew he'd met after he was eighteen, as an adult. It was weird to think of Kurt knowing him when he was young. Like he was reconnecting to his younger self through Kurt.

"Dante!" Pendleton called out, and Jacko's heart sank. Kurt didn't recognize him. Or, worse, didn't remember him.

He tried to smile. "Not Dante, Sheriff. Jacko. Remember me? From Cross?"

Pendleton's eyes narrowed. "Dante?"

"No," Jacko said gently and stepped forward into the oblong rectangle of light. Maybe Pendleton's eyesight had gone. "Not Dante, Sheriff. Jacko. Jacko Jackman."

Pendleton frowned.

This wasn't going well.

Jacko opened his mouth to repeat his name when Pendleton stepped forward, hugged him. When he pulled away, he had tears in his eyes. He held on to Jacko by the shoulders. Jacko remembered him as a big man, but now he was looking down on the sheriff.

"Dante." The sheriff whispered the name and his voice broke. "I'm so sorry. Can you forgive me? It was too dangerous for you to know. You know what they would have done." He was searching Jacko's face for something. For what?

"Okay," Jacko said.

"I kept it from you all those years. I helped keep Sara in the trailer park outside town so no one would see him."

Whoa. What?

"Whenever Villalongo's thugs were around, I made sure they stayed far away from him. I made sure they never saw him." Pendleton held on to Jacko's shoulders tightly, grip surprisingly strong for a geezer. "I protected him as much as I could, I swear. I did everything I could."

His eyes turned shiny, voice cracking with emotion.

Jacko always knew what to do in danger. He had the reaction time of a cobra, his teammates said. Instant and deadly.

But now? With an old guy whose mind was going, was maybe already gone? What the fuck was he supposed to do? The only thing he could. He patted the old guy's back awkwardly.

Under the shirt, he could feel fragile bones covered in loose skin. Pendleton was trembling slightly. For a second, Jacko placed his hand against the old man's back to provide a moment of support. Against his palm, he could feel Pendleton's heart racing, fast and weak.

Pendleton was searching his face. "Your eyes," he whispered.

"It's okay," Jacko said. What else could he say?

"They're different." Pendleton was frowning fiercely now. "Not—not the same. What did you do to your eyes?"

Pendleton was tuning in and out of reality. He was also breathing heavily. Maybe Jacko was somehow stirring him up? Reviving memories the old man couldn't place? Memory loss was the hallmark of dementia.

Pendleton straightened up, pulled away, hands clasping and unclasping. "I should have told you," he said. "It was wrong of me not to. But…it was so dangerous, you know?"

"Yes, of course," Jacko said gravely, playing along. "I know. Look, why don't we sit down for a minute?" *Before your agitation gives you a stroke.*

Pendleton's breathing was fast and uneven now, as if he were running a race and not standing stock still in front of Jacko. Agitation was making his chest rise and fall. A vein throbbed in his temple amid the white hairs. He swayed on his feet. Jacko took Pendleton by the elbow, wanting to lead him to the one chair in the room before he fell down.

But Pendleton resisted, clutching at Jacko's arm. He kept peering at Jacko's face, as if seeing him from a great distance. He cocked his head, frowning. "So…you forgive me? Please say you forgive me."

"Sure," Jacko said easily. "I forgive you. No question. Why don't you just sit down, now? Rest a while."

Pendleton blinked. "But—he might be coming. Right now. For you." And he trembled even harder.

Fuck. What was the old man afraid of? Was he chasing ghosts in his head? Or was it someone *here?* In this facility? Was he being abused?

Jacko looked him over carefully. He didn't have any suspicious bruises, didn't look injured in any way. Jacko took Pendleton's wrist in one hand and with the other, pushed up the shirt sleeve to the shoulder. He examined the arm closely, but there was nothing, no sign of any harm. He did the same to the other arm then examined his neck.

People were manhandled by the neck and arms. Pendleton showed no signs of it.

But he showed signs of other things. His shirt was frayed at the neck and the cuffs, the pants threadbare and too big for him. He'd lost a lot of weight and he had to cinch his ancient belt tight to hold up the pants. He was wearing socks and slippers and Jacko swallowed when he saw a hole in one of his socks.

That son of his wasn't doing his job. If Jacko had had a father like Pendleton, that man sure as hell wouldn't have holes in his socks.

Pendleton was sitting, looking up at him, eyes pleading. "Promise me you'll look after yourself. I couldn't stand it if something happened to you after all these years."

That was easy to promise. Jacko folded the old man's soft hand between his big hard ones. "I promise. I promise to take care of myself."

The old man relaxed, the trembling abating. Whatever memories had him riled up were fading.

Jacko crouched in front of him so they were eye to eye. "Okay, Sheriff. I want you to promise me something now."

Pendleton blinked. "Okay," he said uncertainly.

Jacko pulled out his card case and placed his ASI card in the sheriff's hand. He folded the old, wrinkled hand around it. "On there are my phone numbers. I circled my personal cell number. I want you to promise me that you'll call me if you need anything. Is that clear?"

The sheriff swallowed, nodded.

"Repeat that."

"I call you," Pendleton whispered. "If I need you."

"That's right. I have to go now, but I need to know you'll call if you need something."

"Yes, I will." The sheriff's expression suddenly turned crafty. He tapped the skin beside Jacko's right eye. Jacko didn't like being touched by anyone other than Lauren, but he let it slide. "Contact lenses. That's it. Am I right?"

Jacko didn't sigh though he wanted to. "No, no contact lenses." He rose, put his hand on Pendleton's shoulder. "I have to go," he said again.

Pendleton nodded, head tilted back to watch his eyes. "That's okay. I understand."

Jacko's hand tightened. "And before I go, I just want to say how grateful I am you looked out for me all those years. I appreciate it."

"They never got you," he answered. "All those years and they didn't know. It was the only way to protect you."

Jacko heard the words, but his heart was already pointed toward home. There was some kind of mystery here, but solving it was not as important as getting back to Lauren, where he belonged. At some point in the future he'd come back, maybe with her, and he'd try to figure out what was in the smoky depths of the sheriff's mind. It wasn't that important. What *was* important was to head back home.

"That's fine," he said, though, because the sheriff's face was tight. What he was saying was important to him. Jacko wanted him to know that

LISA MARIE RICE

he was being heard. He didn't understand but that was okay. The next time they'd talk more.

He'd accomplished what he'd wanted. He'd told Sheriff Pendleton how important his help had been for the rough youngster he'd been. Pendleton had believed in him and had given him plenty of second chances. It had made a difference to Jacko because back then, nobody had believed in him. He was Sara Jackman's son and the dregs of the earth.

Pendleton had *seen* him, and Jacko hoped that the sheriff realized that Jacko *saw* him, too. Jacko'd been handicapped by his mom and the sheriff was now handicapped by his illness, but that didn't mean that debts couldn't be repaid.

The sheriff was so diminished right now, it hurt something in Jacko's chest. He'd been such a big man, powerful in his own right, powerful because he wore a badge he believed in. To see him reduced to a quavering old man was painful.

Jacko bent to kiss the sheriff on the forehead and left the room.

Before leaving, he stopped by the admin office. Nurses and other staffers were going in and out. In the middle of a hive of activity was a calm, middle-aged African-American woman who seemed on top of everything.

Jacko stepped in.

"Help you, sir?" she asked, looking at him over reading glasses perched on the end of her nose. LaShawna Johnson was written on a nameplate.

Jack placed his forearms on the desk and leaned in. "Yes, I'd like a word about the patient in room 212."

"Sheriff Pendleton," she nodded.

"Yes. I left him a little...confused."

"Yes. That is very possible. Sheriff Pendleton has a mild form of dementia that is progressing. Sometimes he gets extremely disoriented. We do our best to keep him stable."

Okay, this is where it got a little sticky. "I noticed that he's wearing very old clothes. Is there a reason for that?"

She regarded him thoughtfully. "Green Orchards prides itself on its treatment of patients. They get the finest care in all senses of the term. Even the food is excellent. Their private possessions, though, are their own."

Meaning—*if the dipshit son isn't sending money for decent clothes, it's not our fault.*

Jacko looked her right in the eyes. "Ms. Johnson, Sheriff Pendleton was very kind to me when I was a kid. Would it be possible to leave some money here to be spent on personal things for him? Things that would make him more comfortable? New clothes, for example? An MP3 player. He used to like music a lot. Country and bluegrass. If he doesn't have a music player, I'd like for him to have one."

"Mr...."

"Jackman."

"Mr. Jackman, if you leave money for Sheriff Pendleton, I will personally see to it that it goes to making his life more pleasant. Sheriff Pendleton is a good man, a kind man. Any money you leave would go straight to him. If you leave me your email, I will send you photographs."

"Perfect." Jacko peeled off five one hundred dollar bills and left them on the desk, together with his business card. "You'll find my email and phone numbers on the card. If Sheriff Pendleton needs anything, please call me. I'd also like to send him some money from time to time, if that's possible."

Once, when he was twelve, Pendleton had given Jacko two hundred bucks to cover six months of unpaid bills, otherwise the electric company was going to cut the lights. After that, Jacko started working, doing odd jobs, so he was never without some cash. But that two hundred had saved their bacon during a particularly cold winter.

Pendleton also used to slip Jacko the odd twenty.

Now the tables were turned. Pendleton had only what his son sent, which clearly wasn't much, and Jacko had plenty of money. It felt good to think of making Pendleton's last years more comfortable.

"That's very kind, Mr. Jackman," the clerk said. "Your money will be put to good use. I'll make sure of it personally."

And she would. Jacko knew how to size up people and LaShawna Johnson had the look of kindness about her, coupled with efficiency. He had no doubt every penny would be spent on the sheriff.

"Thank you, ma'am." Jacko shook her hand and walked out of the building, into the soft sunset turning everything a red gold.

He took in a deep breath, filling his lungs with fresh air. The facility was clean, but there was an unmistakable scent of human decay. Nothing like the field hospitals in Afghanistan, of course—full of gore and trauma and smelling of the slaughterhouse. No, this was more like a winding down, a fading away. Something that happened to everyone. Everyone ages, everyone dies.

But right *now*, Jacko was young and healthy and in a great place. He loved Lauren, he loved his job, he was going to be a father. He had his whole life ahead of him. He felt free and light, the painful past shed and discarded, an empty husk behind him.

He pulled out, heading east for the I-5. To Portland it was going to be another fourteen- or fifteen-hour drive.

He'd find a decent motel somewhere in California, have a meal, sleep and shower and get into Portland by early afternoon.

His skin prickled with the desire to get home, but there was no use killing himself. He came back from missions with bruises under his eyes, hollowed out with fatigue. That wasn't how he wanted Lauren to see him.

He'd rest because it was prudent to do so, and so he could come back to her relatively fresh. And unburdened. That light, clean feeling, that sense that he was a new man who'd left a hard past behind him, permeated his being. It felt good.

So he'd drive carefully, rest, and make his way home in a relaxed fashion.

Because, hell, he had all the time in the world.

"Honey, are you *sure?*" Felicity leaned in close, her voice low. No one else could hear. Metal and Joe were in the other room, arguing about the various merits of some kind of fancy new gun.

Felicity had asked already three times.

"I'm sure," Lauren said gently, and put her hand over Felicity's. They were in the kitchen sipping tea and eating slices of the *tarte tatin* Isabel had sent over. Metal and Joe had checked every single system she had—the alarm system, the door locks, the motion sensors, every single faucet, TV and radio reception, even the functioning of her freezer—in hope of finding something they could fix for her. Again, Lauren was almost tempted to break something so they could fix it and feel better.

While the guys did their thing, Felicity sat with her in the kitchen and they talked books and movies and food, avoiding the eight hundred-pound gorilla in the room. Jacko's absence.

Felicity was quivering to help. Help for her wasn't fixing a faucet—she always said she was hopeless at practical stuff. Help for Felicity was tracking down Jacko.

"Aren't you curious to know where he is?" Felicity persisted. Her pretty face was scrunched in a frown. Her friend wasn't usually the prying sort, but she wanted desperately to help Lauren in the only way she could. She'd finally broken down and offered to tell Lauren where Jacko was.

But Lauren didn't want that.

"Yeah, I am." Lauren looked down at the tablecloth, unable to meet Felicity's bright blue eyes. Because Felicity could read how very much she wanted to know. After a moment, she raised her head, looked Felicity full in the face. "But it doesn't feel right. It's Jacko who has to tell me where he is."

Felicity bit her lips. *But he's not telling you where he is. I could do that for you.* The words were right there on her face.

"If you told me, it would be like...like spying."

Felicity bowed her head.

"Wait." Lauren narrowed her eyes. "You know where he is, don't you?"

Felicity sighed. "Yes. I do. I had to follow the cell because Jacko turned the transponder off. Metal says that is a big no-no at ASI."

"So you've been following his cell."

"I have."

"I don't want to know where he's been," Lauren warned.

Felicity dipped her head. "Yeah. Got it."

"He turned the transponder off. That means he doesn't want anyone interfering with him."

Felicity gave a small smile. "I consider that a gesture. Of defiance. He doesn't care that he can be tracked; he just wanted to make it hard to do. It's easy for Metal and the guys to track an ASI transponder, they have an app for that on their computers. The cell is harder. His is encrypted and supposedly untrackable."

"But you can track it," Lauren said. "Right?"

"Right." Felicity wasn't smug. There were very few electronic devices she couldn't track. If it was connected to the net, whether the aboveground one or the dark one, she could track it. It was like she had a sixth sense. Or was "mistress of the dark arts," as some of the ASI guys muttered.

"Honey?" Metal called from the living room.

Felicity stood. "So I guess the guys have finished making your house safe for today. You could survive the apocalypse."

Lauren sighed. She really appreciated what the ASI men did for her, but she'd be glad to have them gone, too. "I'm safe from intruders, from door-to-door salesmen, from bears and from aliens. I'm pretty locked up for the night."

"*And* you have a whole *tarte tatin.*"

"That I do. I could maybe be persuaded to share, if you wanted."

Felicity's eyes rounded. Her fondness for desserts—for sweets of any kind—was legendary, but she liked to eat them in company. Lauren chalked it up to the many years she'd spent closed up in her house, living at her computer without any human company at all. She had plenty of company now, not to mention living with Metal, who took up the space of two people. Lauren would hate her for eating so many sweets and remaining reed-slender, but Felicity was too nice to hate. "Oh, don't tempt me! I can't though," she added, regret rich in her voice. "I've got a freezer full of Isabel's offerings and Metal threatened to take my laptop away if I added any more."

That was a threat with teeth. Felicity without her laptop…that was enough to give anyone the shivers.

Metal and Joe stood in the kitchen doorway. Both were scowling, but Metal's face cleared immediately when he saw Felicity.

"Hey," he said, deep voice soft.

Felicity's pale skin turned faintly pink with pleasure. "Hey back."

Joe scoured the kitchen with his gaze, keenly looking for things to fix. But there was nothing. He looked at Lauren. "So, I think I'll head out."

"More like Isabel's preparing dinner and you want to get there early," Felicity said, with a roll of her eyes.

A corner of his mouth lifted. "That too."

They gathered at the door.

Felicity bent to kiss her cheek. "Remember honey, if you need anything, anything at all—"

"Call us." Metal's eyes were hard.

"Day or night," Joe added.

"Except probably not at mealtimes," Lauren said.

"If you call at mealtimes, there should be guns or blood involved." Felicity laughed and Lauren smiled.

Metal made a gun of his big hand and pointed his index finger at her. "When we leave—"

"Set the alarm." Lauren did *not* roll her eyes, but it took a heroic show of self-control. "Yes, Mom. Will do so immediately."

It was all over the top, but she knew it was love for her and—in a roundabout, half-assed way—love for Jacko, too. They knew Jacko was coming back. They knew—as she knew—that Jacko would have to be dead not to come back, and he was a hard man to kill. They knew he hadn't just disappeared and they knew that whatever he was doing, it was important to him. They also wanted her to let Jacko know they'd looked out for her.

The instant the three were out the door, Lauren set the alarms and sensors. It was not an easy process and for the first week after Jacko had installed it, she'd had to follow written instructions, step by step. There was a fine line, Jacko'd told her, between remembering what to do and paying attention to it. It could easily turn into a rote series of movements but when it became rote, you no longer paid attention and you could skip a step. The subtext being that the instant you let your attention drop, demons would boil up from hell and invade your home.

It was the way the ASI men had operated in the field, and they carried it over into civilian life. Meticulous, incredibly detail-oriented, slightly paranoid.

So Lauren paid attention to setting the code, reactivating the motion sensors, switching on the perimeter lights, activating the IR cameras. Knowing it was overkill, knowing it was all important to Jacko. He'd lived in a dangerous world all his life. Since childhood. He took nothing for granted.

Lauren, too, had felt the rough edge of violence. For two years she'd been on the run, with Jorge on her tail, and it had nearly destroyed her. She was still feeling the effects of living in a state of adrenalin-drenched terror.

She was safe now, in the midst of a group of people who loved her, but those two years had given her an enormous appreciation for the little things in life. Like not being killed.

So she punched in codes and twisted knobs and flipped switches and closed herself in for the night.

She and Jacko had made love so many times, were so physically close, that she sometimes felt the ghost of his essence inside her. And now she was carrying his child, the closest connection possible. It was what had allowed her to remain relatively calm these past days, because she could feel him inside her. If he were hurt in some way, if he'd left her—she'd have felt it. She'd know. She felt an echo of suffering but not physical—emotional. Something he had to face on his own. She'd felt all of that very strongly.

And she could also feel that he was still very far away. She could lock herself in for the night.

Her hand touched the wall to the left of the door. She placed her palm against it, as if to absorb memories through her hand. This—this very spot—was the place Jacko had first kissed her. He'd pressed against her right here and given her the hottest kiss of her life. She'd been hoping for it but not expecting it.

There was a tiny dent in the wall where Jacko'd pressed with all his might to keep from grabbing her hard. His big, powerful hands had pressed the wall on either side of her head, encasing her in a cage of hard, powerful, aroused male. He told her that at that first kiss, he'd been so turned on, he was frightened of touching her. He'd only touched her with his mouth. Just his mouth on hers had almost been enough to give her an orgasm.

The plan had been for one hot night before disappearing completely from Portland because that evening there'd been the possibility that her cover was blown. Which was bad news, considering the psycho who was after her was a step-cousin who'd happily blow her brains out in a second to get what he thought was his rightful share of a criminal empire, courtesy of her mobbed-up stepfather.

Jorge, the step-cousin, had killed two people to get to her, and he'd have killed everyone around her if he had to. Lauren had fallen in love with her friends in Portland…Suzanne, Claire, Allegra. Even the remote chance of Jorge hurting them—she couldn't go there.

Jacko was driving her home from the opening of a show of her artwork, which had turned into her farewell evening in Portland. The plan was to disappear the next day to…she'd had no idea where. Anywhere. Anywhere far away and remote enough to hide from Jorge. Leaving Portland, leaving her friends and, above all, leaving Jacko was breaking her heart.

On that ride across town on a snowy evening—that was when she'd decided to seduce Jacko.

Jacko, the super stud. Jacko, whose sexual exploits were legendary in ASI. Jacko, who liked them hot and young and sexy and for one night only.

Jacko, who was always around her but treated her like his eighty-year-old aunt.

She remembered thinking that this might be her last shot at sex for a long time—maybe the rest of her life—and so having sex with Jacko was fitting. Might as well go out in style. If nothing else, Jacko was guaranteed to give her a good time.

Though she knew she wasn't his type—she was the furthest thing from a hot biker chick—she thought maybe she could convince him to take her to bed. Sort of like a mercy fuck. She'd be gone the next day anyway, disappeared forever. Why not? If she could only coax him into her bed, she wouldn't ask him for anything more. One night and she'd be gone.

Turned out Jacko didn't need much coaxing.

Turned out Jacko had been in love with her and scared of her at the same time. This huge man, a deadly sniper, who could kill a man with his pinkie, this man was terrified of *her*.

He confessed it later to her.

What she'd taken as indifference to her as a woman had been intense interest, and fear of rejection.

Well, in a way, he was right. Under anything but those precise conditions—life under threat but feeling safe with Jacko—she wouldn't have entertained the idea of him as a lover. He was rough-edged, but above all, he was frightening. In her former life, Lauren would not have been able to distinguish between him being a threat to others and him being a threat to her.

Now that she knew him, she knew he could never hurt her, ever. He went out of his way never to use his strength against her. But BJ—Before Jorge—when life had been normal, she wouldn't have taken the trouble to look beyond Jacko's rough exterior. Beyond the shaved head and the tats and the piercings and the oversized muscles.

She would have missed the fact that he was an amazingly intelligent and observant and patient man. He was a man who'd taken the worst life could throw at him and had prevailed. He was a man who loved how she introduced him to fine art and classical music. He reacted instinctively to art, this man who'd been brought up in a semi-feral state.

So in a roundabout way, Lauren was grateful to that monstrous cokehead of a step-cousin, because without him threatening her life, she'd never have met Jacko, and would certainly never have appreciated him.

She ran her palm over the wall next to the door, surprised at the lack of scorch marks. Jacko's first kiss had been that hot. The hottest she'd ever had, bar none. It was a wonder her head hadn't exploded.

In that instant, for the very first time in two years, she hadn't felt hunted and alone and afraid. She was being kissed by the strongest man she'd ever seen and Jorge had simply disappeared from her head.

Ah, that night had changed her life forever.

When they'd talked about it afterward, Jacko made fun of the difference between men and women. Everyone knew he was hot for her, except her. She hadn't understood that he was "dragging his dick around after her," as he so colorfully put it. She hadn't got that, no clue at all.

Smiling, Lauren made herself a cup of hot milk and drifted into the bedroom. Their bedroom. Though it was full of frills, with silver potpourri holders and flower vases, and a lovely fragile nursing chair that Jacko never, ever sat on, and flowered curtains and a big, ornate chest of drawers, he never complained. It was the furthest thing from a Jacko-room possible, but he had adapted. Took it like, well, a man.

They'd made love countless times in this room. It was their secret bower. She'd been incredibly happy here with Jacko and she would be again.

She'd grown addicted to feeling his huge body next to hers under the covers, generating immense heat. This summer she was going to have to put in air conditioning because she'd be damned if she'd give up sleeping holding on to him.

As Lauren slipped between the perfumed sheets, she caressed her belly and thought of Jacko. He'd shown his love for her over and over in this room, in this bed.

And that first night—

Her eyes closed and she gave a long sigh.

They'd undressed in the dark in her bedroom, just the light from the streetlamps outside casting a faint glow. He'd undressed her slowly, confessing later that he'd had to clamp down on himself to keep from tearing all her clothes off and tossing her on the bed.

That first time, Jacko was all about control. Every line of his body was restrained. The tendons in his neck had been taut, forearm muscles so tight she could see the overlay of musculature as he unbuttoned, snapped open.

The thing she'd noticed that betrayed his tension had been that his hands trembled. A famous sniper's hands were trembling. It hadn't been visible but she'd felt it when he'd covered her naked breasts with his big hands.

Later he'd told her he was not only frightened of somehow hurting her in his excitement, but scared he might rip her underwear. Quite right. She'd been wearing a La Perla bra and panties. But she'd been frightened too. That Jorge would come after her, that she was going to have to leave her wonderful life and wonderful friends in Portland. That she would live the rest of her life keeping her

173

head low, never making friends, constantly on the run.

And frightened that however many precautions she might take, she'd one day make a mistake and he would find her and kill her. And she would die alone and unloved.

Lauren smiled. Jacko, that night, had loved her right out of her fear and panic, had filled her head and body with heat, with power.

She remembered undressing him. He'd let her undress him so she'd feel she had power. But she'd felt that anyway. His entire body—strong and powerful—had been placed at her service. He didn't make a move until she initiated it.

That first sight of him naked—wow. Amazing. He worked out but he didn't have those swollen, artificial-looking muscles bodybuilders sported. He just looked like he'd been born strong and had kept himself in shape. And those tattoos…God. She knew he had tattoos—barbed wire tats around his wrists. They'd been sexy enough. But he had a huge tribal tattoo covering one shoulder, flowing down over his chest, a swirl encircling a nipple.

Her vagina had contracted when she'd seen that, a totally involuntary reaction of her body to this amazingly strong and virile man. His body had reacted too. When her gaze raked down over his chest down to his groin, to his amazingly large and erect penis, her look alone had made him bigger, thicker. He'd swelled impossibly when she confessed she hadn't had sex in a long while.

Being on the run for your life would do that.

And the first thing he'd said was that he didn't want to hurt her. He'd been as gentle as possible that first time. Gentle and tender and loving.

After which they'd had sex so hot, it should have been illegal.

God.

She missed him so much. With anyone else, she might have pleasured herself into sleep. It was what she'd done those two years hiding from Jorge. Sometimes when she was particularly lonely or particularly afraid, with no one to hold her, she'd touch herself until she had a short orgasm. Like a little blip on radar. Nothing like what Jacko gave her.

She couldn't touch herself now, not even missing him so very much. It was as if her body belonged to him.

But she was attuned to him, and she felt something change, like a change in the molecules of the air. A lodestone shifting. The center of her universe aligning.

Jacko was coming back to her. She could feel it. Soon, he would be back with her and her world would be complete. Smiling, Lauren slipped gently into sleep.

In a Motel 6 outside Fresno, California

Jacko's eyes opened suddenly. Like all SEALs he'd been trained to be instantly alert and aware upon awakening. He lay still, as he always did. In the field, making noise when waking up could be fatal. More times than he could count he'd waited in a hide for days to take a shot. Once, he'd hidden in a tree for three days. So he'd trained himself to wake up and remain still.

There was something about waking up now…he looked around, moving only his eyes. A motel room. Motel, not hotel. He could hear highway noises right outside his window. The room smelled clean, looked entirely anonymous by the lights of the streetlamps outside filtering in through the thin curtains.

Nothing strange about the room.

He hadn't dreamed. That was it. These past nights his sleep had been restless and he'd had nightmares every time he'd closed his eyes. Monsters killing Lauren, Lauren dying, blood and pain. He'd woken up sweating and terrified. He was never terrified, not while awake anyway. These dreams—these nightmares—caught him by surprise, with creatures boiling up from the depths of his subconscious, representing his deepest terror. The terror of losing Lauren.

Right now he felt…fine. More than fine. He'd slept enough to feel rested, and he was ready to get back on the road.

More than anything else, though, he felt happy. Happier even than these past months of living with Lauren, which had been just amazing. Because, well, there was going to be more of that. The rest of his life, in fact. And there was going to be a child.

For the very first time, panic didn't fill his head at that thought.

A kid. His kid and Lauren's kid. Man.

A girl. *A little girl.* A ferocious desire for a little girl rose up in him, fierce and unstoppable and huge. A little girl. Small and delicate, like Lauren. Beautiful and smart. Oh God, he'd get to watch her grow up. Love her and protect her, make sure she was raised by two loving parents. And the ASI family—she'd have a billion affectionate aunts and uncles. Cousins coming out of her ears because Joe and Isabel were already talking about having kids, as were Metal and Felicity. It was early for Jack and Summer, but Jack had grown up in a big, loving family and he'd want kids. A lot of them.

Jacko could see it. A passel of kids, swarming in and out of each other's houses.

Before Lauren, none of this would have held any appeal to him, none at all. Kids were liabilities, walking pieces of your heart right out there in the open, subject to life's violence and pain. Like having hostages just waiting for enemies to use against you.

But right now, Jacko didn't have any enemies. Lauren didn't either. All they had around them were friends, people who cared about them. Who'd care for their kid, too.

Jacko had never seen the need for families. As far as he could tell, families were there to fuck people up. Shrinks wouldn't have a job if families weren't so crappy. Jacko had made the Navy his family and it had worked out just fine. So a family of his own hadn't been in the cards. Hadn't even been on the horizon

And then Lauren had come along and changed everything.

It was dark outside. It was barely four in the morning. He had a little under twelve hours of driving to go, but Jacko lay in bed, totally relaxed, staring up at the dark ceiling and letting the thought of their child wash over him. He saw scenes—holding a little newborn. Her first steps, running into his arms. He'd measure his life not by how old he was getting, but by how much she was growing.

A whole lifetime of love, with Lauren and their kid. More kids, too. Why the hell not? Yeah. A big family. Wouldn't that be a kick in the ass? Jacko Jackman, head of a clan.

Well, stranger things had happened.

The thought was weird but not repellant. Nothing was repellant about his life, actually. He had a great woman, a great job. He had plenty of money and was surrounded by friends. And he was going to be a father.

None of this had been even remotely in his head when he'd joined the Navy. He'd enlisted as soon as legally possible, hoping only to get away from his mother, get out of Cross. Mostly he'd been hoping to be among people who weren't killing themselves slowly. He wanted to be among people who weren't messed up. The bar was low as far as his ambitions went.

Get out of Cross. Stay alive. Have three squares a day and a bed. Three hots and a cot, as they used to say.

And now look at him.

The future didn't just look bright, it beckoned to him. Good times ahead and people with him to share the bad times. A family. A nuclear family that was all his. And a broader one, of people who cared for him.

There were no shadows left in him at all. Not even the ones he'd carried with him all his life. He felt freed of ancient hurts, like slipping off handcuffs and chains that he'd been dragging around since childhood.

For the first time in his life, he felt safe. Not because the world had become a better place, no way. The world was shitty. Always had been, always would be. He felt safe because he had people to love and who loved him and he had people at his back, just as he had theirs.

It was still dark but he was raring to go. There was a coffee machine and vending machine selling pure crap in the lobby. He'd grab a bad coffee and something filled with chemicals and get going. Lauren would have a heart attack if she knew he was loading up on carbs and chemicals, but it would shave some time off the trip. Later he'd stop at a drive-through and get a burger and fries.

Nothing like the spectacular food he got at home. But still, he had the rest of his life to eat healthy. Right now, all he wanted was to make good time.

Jacko was revved to the max.

Time to go home.

Green Orchards Retirement Home

There was a whole goddamn weather system in his head. Sometimes it was foggy and rainy and sometimes the sun came out. This morning, the sun was out and he could see clearly. Think clearly. He'd been agitated last night and they'd upped his dosage of the pills they thought kept him calm, but they didn't. They just made him confused.

Kurt Pendleton knew when to take the pills and when not to. Last night, he didn't. And this morning he could think straight.

Yesterday had been a shock that rocked him. The man he'd known and admired so many years ago, here to see him. But damn, it wasn't *him*. Dante Jimenez. Pendleton couldn't figure it out. The man was right there in front of him but…not. And he wasn't responding the way he was supposed to.

Pendleton admired Jimenez, always had. A law enforcement legend and the best agent the DEA ever had. The man had had a dangerous job and had cojones big as boulders to go in undercover and rise through the ranks until he became old man Villalongo's right-hand man. And Carlos Villalongo had spent so many years trying to get revenge. He'd kill—and he *had* killed—to get a bead on Dante.

If he'd had even a breath of suspicion that Dante had a son…

Pendleton had worked hard, trying to protect Dante all these years, hadn't he? He'd hid Jacko from the Villalongo clan and then rushed Jacko away from Cross as soon as he could legally join the military. And here Dante was. Except he wasn't. Dante but not Dante.

The puzzle kept him awake most of the night. And then the clouds parted and he could see the entire picture.

Not Jimenez. His son, Jacko. All grown up and the spitting image of his famous father. Who knew nothing about him.

That secret that had burned a hole in his heart for the past—how many years was it? He tried to calculate it but gave up. A long time, that was the answer. He'd kept the secret a long time.

Maybe too long.

Maybe the son coming to see him was a sign that he should let go.

He knew that the clouds in his head came more often now, created a thicker fog every time they came. The time would come when—Pendleton looked at it clearly for the first time—when he wouldn't have the option of telling Jimenez because he wouldn't remember.

Pendleton was the only one who knew. The only one in the world who could unite these two after so many years. The only one who could right a wrong decades old. Once he was gone, it would be lost. Jacko would never know who his father was. Dante would never know he had a son.

In the years during which he'd sheltered the young boy, Pendleton had been certain he was doing the right thing. The boy would have been in deadly danger if it was known he was Dante Jimenez's son. But the man he'd seen, the man who was the spitting image of his father, looked tough as nails. A hard man to kill, just as his father was.

Already he could feel the encroaching darkness at the edges of his mind. By this afternoon, he would be lost. How many times could he come back? Maybe this was his last shot at clearheadedness, the last time he could do this.

And if not today, soon. Because soon the clouds would eat him up and there would be only darkness.

A tear tracked down his weather-beaten face. That was something else about this goddamned thing he had. His emotions—they were all over the goddamned place. At times it felt like he was drowning in feelings he couldn't control. They shook him like a hurricane, blinding him to the outside world.

Shame, fear, panic—they roiled inside him, an unstoppable storm.

He came to in his chair, starting awake. The storm was over, the clouds gone. Peering at his watch, he saw two hours had gone by. The periods of clarity were becoming shorter and shorter. Soon, he knew, they would be gone forever.

Use this time while you can, he thought. Because maybe he'd been wrong about keeping the truth from Jimenez. The boy had suffered, that was for sure.

Though the man who'd visited him didn't look like he was suffering. He'd turned into a fine man, just like his father.

It was time they knew.

He had to do this while the clouds were gone.

There was a number he could call. Jimenez had given it to him a long time ago. Pendleton hadn't left the number with his successor because there was the reward floating in the air for any news regarding Jimenez. The man who became sheriff after him would have sold his best friend down the river for half a million dollars.

Constable, the one who came after his successor, was even worse. He would have sold his *mother* down the river for half a million dollars. Nobody could have the number he was about to call.

He still had it. A crumpled piece of paper Dante Jimenez had thrust into his hand at the last minute. *Call me any time you need something, man.*

Pendleton had never needed to use that number. But now he did. He needed to help his old friend.

All these years, he thought he'd been protecting Jimenez. Villalongo was a monster. But Jimenez was smart and tough and his son looked like he could handle himself, too. It was a risk, but then life was a risk. And soon he wouldn't be able to do this.

Let them sort it out.

The crumpled piece of paper was in his wallet, had been for over thirty years.

Time to tell the finest man he'd ever known that he had a son, and that Pendleton had kept that info from him.

His hands shook as he punched in the number. It was a secret number at the DEA, the number for the case officers directing undercover agents. Three generations would have passed through that office. Pendleton didn't even know if Dante was retired. But everyone would know Dante. He was a legend.

"Hello," he said when someone picked up the phone at the other end without identifying himself. Pendleton hated how his voice shook. *Onset of Parkinson's* his doctor had said. "I have a message for Dante Jimenez. It's urgent."

CHAPTER EIGHT

Portland

As the sun set behind the oak trees lining her street, Lauren closed the door with a sigh, punched in the alarm codes and leaned her back against the wall.

The girls had come out in force and had spent lunch here, bless them. Felicity, Isabel and Summer. Metal, Joe and Jack were out of town for the day on ASI business and their women had come over for an extended brunch that lasted all afternoon. Isabel had brought a pasta casserole and a chocolate and pear cake, and Felicity and Summer, who didn't cook, brought cheeses and grapes.

They'd eaten until the sun started sinking and then had broken out a bottle of Pinot Grigio Summer brought. Lauren refrained but had fun watching them. Isabel, Felicity and Summer had gotten a little sloshed and had laughed a lot.

Lauren'd had a good time but she was glad to be alone once more. The only person she wanted now was Jacko.

She'd put up a brave front but the truth was, she was worried.

Jacko hadn't called in twenty-four hours. Those calls where he couldn't talk? With hindsight they were reassuring. He was keeping in touch in his own way. But now it was like he'd disappeared off the map and the last tenuous tie she had with him had severed.

Felicity had gently taken Lauren aside and murmured once again that she could track Jacko, find out where he was. But that felt wrong. It felt like cheating, like admitting she didn't trust Jacko. She did. She trusted Jacko with her heart and with her life.

So she'd said no and Felicity had simply nodded her head. "Okay, no tracking," she whispered. If Felicity said she wouldn't track, she wouldn't.

For the first time, Lauren wondered whether she should just let Felicity do her thing. What would it hurt? Just to know where Jacko was, to reassure herself?

But then, what if she didn't want to know the answer? What if—what if Jacko was gone? Really truly gone? What if he'd left her? A couple of days ago she would have sworn in blood that Jacko would never leave her. That he was hers for life.

But that was before she'd seen his face when he'd discovered that she was pregnant.

That hadn't been joy she saw in his face. He looked stricken, almost wounded. Jacko—the strongest man she'd ever seen—looked like he'd been brought to his knees by one blow.

Strength wasn't always enough. Her Jacko wasn't indestructible. Her Jacko had demons in him. When he'd said he knew peace for the first time with her, she'd believed him. But demons had a way of rearing up from nowhere.

What if his demons chased him away from her?

What then?

She was sitting on her kitchen chair, looking down at the pretty tablecloth. Felicity, Isabel and Summer had cleaned up, loaded the dishwasher, put things away, bless them. She should get up, turn the dishwasher on, put some music on, put some soup on for later. Look at the book cover design that was three days overdue and which she hadn't touched. Go over her accounts for her business's bookkeeper, way behind on that. Answer the emails of two families who wanted watercolors of their homes and were willing to pay premium rates.

So much to do. So little desire to do it.

Lauren felt drained of all energy. Maybe it was the baby. All the books said that the first trimester was the worst. She hadn't had morning sickness but she was tired all the time. So sure, that must be it. The pregnancy.

No, that wasn't it. The truth was—she missed Jacko and she was terrified that she had lost him.

Was he coming back?

Or was he gone?

The living room was dark, the only light coming from the kitchen. She was closed up in her cocoon, something she loved. She especially loved it when she was closed in the cocoon with Jacko. But he wasn't here.

He'd never liked staying home, he told her once. Four walls made him feel trapped. Rather than stay home, he'd go out no matter what the weather. Go to some bar and drink and play pool. Go hiking. Take his bike out. Anything.

He didn't say, but she understood that he hadn't liked staying home as a child because he'd lived in a trailer that was a chaotic mess with a crazy drug addict mother. As an adult, he'd had no clue how to create a home. Man, his place had been a study in sensory deprivation. Huge bed, huge couch, huge TV. Stove and fridge and table and two chairs. That was about it. She'd never told him that she found his place profoundly depressing.

He never felt trapped in this house. It was super-feminine but he could do his things just fine. He tinkered with his bike in the garage, where he had a complete workshop with tools she'd never even seen before. The kitchen-dining room was big enough to contain his friends when it was their turn to host the poker parties where Jacko inevitably lost to Joe Harris.

He could listen to all the heavy metal he wanted with his headset. The back room was fitted out to be a gym and he spent hours in there. Preferred it now, he'd said more than once, to the gym he used to go to.

They had their own little world in this house and it was like a kingdom for just the two of them.

How could she stand it if their kingdom was lost, shattered? In such a short time, Jacko had filled her life. How could she live without him? How could she raise their child without him?

Something wet splashed on her hand and she looked down. It was too dark to see what it was but she knew anyway. It was a tear, followed by another one.

God, she'd cried plenty when she was on the run. She'd spent those two horrible years in a succession of cheap motels and rented rooms. Until Felicity made her rock-solid IDs, she never stayed where she had to show ID. So she'd spent days and nights in cheap, depressing places, lonely as hell. Sometimes not speaking to anyone for days, feeling like the only human left alive on earth.

That could never happen now, because she was going to have a child. The only human related by blood to her on earth. It would be Jacko's only blood relation, too.

Had he thought of that? Of this child being *his* flesh and blood? Neither of them had any family. They were each other's family. And now they would be linked by blood.

Unless Jacko couldn't bear it.

Unless Jacko was gone.

His ASI buddies wouldn't let him disappear. They'd track him down wherever he went and would go after him, but Lauren didn't want that. She didn't want a resentful partner who'd been dragged back to her.

She wanted her loving Jacko back, the one who said he'd rather be with her than with anyone else in the world.

Another tear dropped on her hand.

Maybe that Jacko was gone forever.

She dropped her head in her hands, tears trickling through her fingers. This was breaking her heart.

"Don't cry, honey," a deep voice said. The kind of voice that was so deep it reverberated in her diaphragm. The voice that reverberated in her heart.

Lauren lifted her head, saw a dark, broad shape. Her heart thumped hard in her chest.

"God." Jacko sat down beside her, pulled her into his arms. "Don't cry. I can't stand it. Don't cry honey, please."

It was like opening floodgates. Lauren's chest contracted as if someone had punched her and she couldn't breathe. Another sharp pulse in her chest. All her pain and desolation and—yes—fury came boiling up from deep inside her. Tears sprang from her eyes and she trembled and shook as sobs overcame her.

Jacko folded her into him, rested his cheek against the top of her head and held her through the storm.

He was here. Jacko had come back to her. Everything she had repressed—all the anguish and fear—came bubbling out in sobs that racked her body, shook her bones. There was no controlling it; she could barely breathe as she cried her terror out. Jacko didn't say a word, simply held her tightly, one big arm around her waist, one big hand holding the back of her head.

The storm finally passed, leaving Lauren limp in his arms. He was still dressed for the outside; she could smell the cold air and rain on him. Her tears wet his leather jacket, mixing with the raindrops.

She lay against him, spent. Oh God, she'd forgotten how broad he was, how strong. How leaning against him felt like leaning against a mountain, something immovable and forever. She shuddered at the thought that if he hadn't come back, she'd never hold him again. When Jacko felt her shudder, he tightened his hold.

Lauren's head was against his massive shoulder. She turned her head slightly and kissed his neck gently. Her eyes were closed. If this was a mirage, she didn't want to know.

"I was so afraid you weren't coming back," she whispered against his skin.

"I know." His voice was so deep, she felt the vibrations more than heard the words.

"I don't know what I would have done if you hadn't come back," she confessed. In college, she and her girlfriends had always played it cool. They had rules and they stuck by them. Never *ever* let the guy know you cared. She used to go out of her way to avoid talking to someone she slept with, and be unavailable for a few days. Showing your emotions was vastly uncool and Lauren—who was Anne Lowell back then—was never uncool. She knew how to play the game.

But Jacko—there were no games to be played with Jacko. She didn't want to lie to him or hide what was in her heart, ever.

"I know," he said again, and that huge chest lifted on a sigh.

"Are you going to stay?" Lauren's voice came out small.

"Fuck yeah." Now she *knew* he was deeply emotional. Jacko made a real effort to clean his language up in her presence. The f-bomb sometimes escaped but not often. "Forever. You can count on that. I'm going to stay forever. As they say—till death do us part."

Her lips curved in a smile against his chest.

"Speaking of which…" Jacko pulled back and held her away from him. His hands were firm on her shoulders.

"Yeah?"

"Speaking of which, now that you're pregnant, I hope you're finally going to make an honest man out of me."

She stared at him blankly.

"I've had this for a long time now. Waiting for the right moment." He reached into his pocket and brought a box out, offering it to her on his big palm. It was a jewelry box. She knew what was in it. She placed her hand on the top but didn't take it, didn't open it.

Jacko looked at their hands, with the jewelry box between them, then looked deeply into her eyes.

"Lauren Dare, will you do me the honor of marrying me?"

She took in a deep breath and he held a finger up.

"And just to make it complete—Anne Lowell, will you do me the honor of marrying me?"

That earned him a small smile. "I thought we already settled this."

"No," Jacko said, shaking his head while holding her gaze. "We haven't. I've asked before, or at least tried to."

"I didn't say no."

"You didn't say yes, either. Not saying yes is a 'no' in my book."

She was silent, watching his eyes. She wanted to understand what was going on with him. Jacko had the reputation of being inscrutable and in the beginning, before they became lovers, she thought he was a complete enigma. His dark features never betrayed what he was thinking, feeling. He could have come from the moon for all she understood of him.

And then she fell in love with him and now she could read him, inside out.

She knew his entire personality was based on three elements, two old, one new. Loyalty. He was incredibly loyal to his colleagues, to his company. Duty. Jacko was stoic and had duty built into his DNA. If he thought he had to do it, he did it, no matter the cost.

And lastly, love for her. She knew that was now a cornerstone of who he was.

She'd wanted to wait. It seemed insane to her now that she'd wanted to wait. Wait for what? She'd thought they had all the time in the world, but that wasn't true. They were blessed because out of seven billion people in the world, they'd found each other. That had been whatever you wanted to call it. Luck. Fate. Destiny. Whatever the force that had brought them together, it had been powerful.

But there were many other forces at work in the universe that were not benign. She could lose

Jacko. Though his job wasn't as dangerous as being a SEAL, the ASI men often walked into danger without blinking. Jacko drove everywhere. He was an excellent driver but there were literally millions of crazy people on the road, many of them drunk or high. Sometimes both. She could have lost him on this last road trip, wherever it was he'd gone.

No one is immune to illness. However strong Jacko was, cancer was stronger. He could have a heart attack, he could be shot, he could be run over. Anything could rip him from her, in the blink of an eye. No one had immunity from life's dangers. He could be gone in a heartbeat.

This was a very rare man, a man in a million.

There was no waiting.

"Yes," she said, and his face changed. Transformed utterly.

"Yes," he said, and laughed.

Lauren's eyes opened wide. She'd never heard Jacko laugh, ever. He smiled sometimes. Rarely. The laugh was charming and it took ten years off his face. Jacko stood up, hands out. She took his hands and he lifted her up off the couch and into his arms, swinging her about, head back, laughing.

"Yes, yes, *yes!*" he boomed. He held her up so that she was looking down into his face. That dark, beloved face. "When?"

"What?"

"Set the date." He lifted her even higher as she braced her hands against his shoulders. "Not letting you down until you set a date. Soon, too. My kid is going to be born to married parents— and to parents who weren't married a day before the birth. So—soon."

"Soon? How soon?"

"Tomorrow if we could."

He was holding her up as if she were weightless, but she felt light anyway. As if burdens as heavy as boulders had suddenly cracked open and blown away. She hadn't had doubts before, but the fact was that her family hadn't specialized in happy marriages or happy endings. And Jacko's poor mother had led a tragic life. No happy endings for her either. So she'd wondered whether they'd somehow inherited bad marriage genes.

But no. No one's life was predestined. Fate didn't have to thwart them. It wasn't written in the stars that their marriage would fall apart just because she and Jacko came from unhappy backgrounds. They were going to break the mold and work hard at forging happy lives together.

In order to have a happy married life, though, they'd have to be married first. "I don't think we could do that unless we eloped to Vegas."

Jacko opened his mouth and Lauren put a finger across his lips. "Nope. Don't say it. Don't even think it. If we elope, we will never be able to come back here. Everybody would be so angry."

He shrugged a massive shoulder.

"And Isabel wouldn't help plan our wedding reception."

Jacko's eyes widened.

"Yeah." It was a threat with teeth. No one ever wanted to celebrate anything without Isabel helping to plan it. The woman was magic.

"Huh." Jacko shook his head, still holding her up. "That's something to consider, I guess. So set the date. Any date. Right now."

"Okay." Lauren smiled down at him, at that dark, unhandsome face, her heart overflowing. "June 1st. I want to be a June bride. And I won't be showing that much in early June. Is that okay with you?"

"Well, if it can't be tomorrow, then June 1st sounds fine."

Jacko held her close. He was massively erect. She could tell he was aroused by other signs, too, signs she was familiar with. The skin over his cheekbones was darker, his lips were darker too, and fuller. He was watching her with a heavy-lidded gaze, which in her experience led straight to mind-blowing sex.

She lowered her gaze back to his mouth, dropping her head to his, wanting one of Jacko's amazing kisses.

He stopped her an inch from his mouth, holding her up and slightly away from him. "Uh-uh. Not quite yet. So you, Lauren Dare, swear to marry me on June 1st, right?"

She smiled, cocked her head as she studied him. "Right."

He put her on her feet and took her left hand. He watched her eyes as he slid the ring onto her ring finger. He didn't have to look at what he was doing. Jacko was one of the most skilled snipers in the world. He could field strip his rifle in the dark in forty seconds, he could slip a ring on her finger without watching what he was doing.

It was Lauren whose gaze drifted down to her hand. Her eyes widened. It was absolutely perfect. A circle of small diamonds flanked by two sapphires in an exquisite setting.

"So beautiful," Lauren breathed and looked up into Jacko's smiling face. "It must have cost a fortune."

He lifted a shoulder. Jacko didn't care about money, and in any event, he had plenty.

"Who helped you choose it? Suzanne?"

"Bingo." Jacko shook his head. "Man, I was in a sweat. All I knew was that I wanted something special for you. But it was repeated to me over and over that it wasn't just a question of money and size. That you didn't like 'gaudy.' That's Suzanne talking, not me. The hell I know about *gaudy*?"

Lauren suddenly saw how it had played out. "You'd already picked something and Suzanne nixed it."

He winced. "Yeah. That's when the g-word was used. A lot. Isabel chimed in too."

Isabel had been born into one of the top families in America and like Suzanne, she oozed class from her fingertips to her toes. Suzanne and Isabel were, together, an unstoppable force for elegance. It was like they'd invented the concept.

Lauren admired the gorgeous ring on her finger. "What was your original choice?"

Jacko sighed. "Just a rock. The biggest I could find. Suzanne made me take it back. That jeweler was one unhappy puppy, let me tell you."

Lauren smiled up at him. "Well, this one is absolutely perfect. I can wear it while drawing, too. And it's beautiful but I don't need a security guard walking around with me."

"That's more or less what Suzanne said. She said the one I picked out was too heavy. That you wouldn't be able to wear it for ordinary chores and you'd keep taking it off. And I want that ring on your finger every day of your life."

Lauren curled the fingers of her right hand around the fingers of her left, as if someone could take her ring away. She already loved it.

"So, it's a deal?" Jacko nudged her with his shoulder. "Ring, marriage on the first of June, kid already started…we're good?"

"Yeah," Lauren whispered, throat tight. Her eyes were wet and a tear spilled over, ran down her cheekbone. "We're good."

"Whoa." Jacko looked alarmed, which was alarming in itself. He never looked alarmed. But right now he was scowling, the whites of his eyes showing, the skin around his nostrils pale. "You're crying. Why are you crying? Oh fuck, oh fuck." His voice was hoarse as he patted her all over, as if looking for sudden bullet wounds. "What's the matter, honey? Is the thought of being married to me so bad?"

Lauren shook her head and leaned into him, arms outspread. She nestled against him, against that broad chest that was her protection against the world, and held him tightly.

Jacko stopped talking. She was leaning into him, not leaning away. He understood that maybe something was wrong, but that something wasn't her wanting to leave him. So he shut up and held her, which was exactly what she needed.

The tears dried up fast. Hard to cry when Jacko Jackman was holding you tight.

His leather jacket was open and she wiped her wet face against his shoulder. "I'm getting some mascara on your shirt."

"Like I care?" he rumbled, and tightened his hold.

She gave a watery laugh, tipped her head back to look at him, then leaned her forehead against his chest.

She held on to his shirt, now dampened by her tears. The tears had dried up, though. Lauren had a sudden vision—like the curtains over the world were suddenly pulled back. She knew, without any doubt, that these were the last tears she would shed for a long, long while. She could feel it, as surely as she could feel spring in the air outside. For a little while, the sad years were over.

"Those two years I was running," she said finally, voice quiet. "I didn't dare make friends with anyone and I felt so alone. I never knew whether Jorge would find me, and kill someone else while trying to get to me. He'd already killed two women he thought were me, I just couldn't risk it. And I couldn't risk dating anyone. I couldn't tell anyone who I really was. I had to keep the lowest possible profile. You were an anomaly because you just sort of stuck around. Couldn't get rid of you." His arms tightened even further. "And I think in my heart of hearts, I was sure you could handle yourself if Jorge came with his goons."

"Damn right," he muttered.

"But until you, I just assumed that my life was over and I was going to be in hiding until I got old and finally died. And that a husband, a child—a family—were never going to be possible for me. Jorge had taken that away from me. I was so lonely. I cried myself to sleep more times than I can count. I'd spend weeks without talking to anyone other than the guy at the convenience store where I bought milk and bread. All those things—a home and a family. People I could love and who loved me. They were impossible dreams."

She stood straighter as she reached up and cupped Jacko's strong jaw. His jaw muscles bunched under her hand. "And now look at me. At us. We're going to be married, Jacko. We're going to have a child together. Things I thought I'd never have, things I thought were beyond my reach forever, and now I will have them. *We* will have them. It feels like…like being reborn. It feels like magic."

"Sometimes—" Jacko stopped.

"Sometimes what, darling?"

"Sometimes you *can* get what you want." He shook his head and smiled. *You can't always get what you want.* The Rolling Stones line was one of his favorites, summing up his worldview, and he'd just turned it on its head. A complete turnaround in his personal philosophy. "Weird, huh?"

Lauren watched his eyes. "Are you going to tell me where you were and what you did?"

His gaze never wavered from hers. "Of course. Tell you everything. Actually sort of interesting. Found out some stuff."

His speech got clipped when he was emotional. It had taken her a while to realize that. She cupped her hand around his jaw again. "I'm dying to hear it. To hear what happened to you, what you found out."

Jacko nodded. "But first, a shower." He sniffed his armpit and gave an exaggerated shudder. "Been driving a long time." His face changed again, sharpened, eyes focused on her with a laser-like intensity. "We should shower together. You like that."

She did. Showering with Jacko was…whew.

Heat suddenly shimmered through her body, a bright, delicate wave of it starting from her head and moving down. She was flushed pink, she could feel it. Jacko didn't signal things through his skin, it was too dark, too tough. By the time she could see a flush along his cheeks and his lips suffused with blood, he was heavily aroused and ready. Her skin showed everything, immediately. It was a curse.

Jacko was studying her face. "You like that idea," he said again.

No use pretending. "Yeah. You always make showering together…interesting." Which was code for red-hot sex.

He was already shepherding her toward the bedroom and the bathroom beyond. "Now," he said. His face was tight, eyes narrowly focused on her. When he was down to one-syllable words, that meant she was in for a wild ride.

Jacko turned her toward him and started undressing her, utterly concentrated on it. He was quick. Sweater, bra, leggings, panties, lace socks, flats. In about ten seconds Lauren was standing naked in front of him, shivering at what she saw in his eyes.

He frowned and shot a glance at the thermostat. They kept the house slightly colder than normal when he was home, but she'd kept it at 74° in his absence. "You cold?"

"No," she whispered. "Excited."

Jacko closed his eyes tightly for a second and, hands a blur, tore his own clothes off, ushering her into the bathroom with a hand to her bare back. Oh God, she shivered again, just at the feel of his hand against her skin, hot and huge, like a brand. This time he didn't ask if she was feeling hot or cold or was comfortable or uncomfortable. He knew what she was feeling.

A twist of his hand and the shower came on, just as they both liked it—boiling hot. They stepped inside. It was a normal shower, not one of those huge fancy ones, and Jacko took up most of the space. That was okay. Lauren loved being in this enclosed, steamy space with him, their own damp bower.

"Here." Jacko picked up her shower gel and put it in her hand. "Do me." The gleam in his dark eyes showed that he understood exactly the double meaning.

"You sure?" Lauren squirted a dollop of the pink gel into her palm. It was freesia-scented and Jacko said it smelled like pure girl. It did. They had his and her shower gels on the stone tray. His smelled of pine. Because they didn't make engine-oil-scented shower gel.

"I'm sure." Jacko's eyes never left hers. "I want to smell like you."

She shook her head, smiling. "I think for that you need my jasmine-scented body oil and rose-scented body lotion, and your nightwear should be in a drawer that has lavender sachets and…"

He bent and stopped her mouth with his, moving forward two steps until her back was against the glass wall. His mouth moved over hers, tongue deep inside, stroking hers. Her nose was against his cheek, which was slightly bristly. The taste of him was familiar and yet exciting. How was that? The excitement never died down, no matter how many times he kissed her, and he kissed her a lot. He kissed her mouth often, but he also kissed her neck, her breasts, her belly. He kissed her between the thighs exactly as if it were her mouth, tongue deep inside her.

It never got stale. In fact, it got hotter each time because beyond the kiss right now, she remembered those other thousand kisses. Her sex clenched as she remembered his lips there. He could make her come with his mouth alone.

Lauren opened her arms and embraced him. Her hand was full of gel so she spread it over that wide, strong back. How she loved touching him here. Each muscle distinct, so hard she could never make indents with her fingers.

He left her lips and she was about ready to complain when he kissed her behind the ear. Right…there. Which to her astonishment, had turned out to be an erogenous zone. Big time.

She'd never known that. And it turned out that the tendons of her neck were erogenous zones, too, and made her shiver when he ran his lips up and down them. And when he bit her, right on the spot where her neck met her shoulder…well, that turned out to be a huge turn-on.

If you'd told her two years ago that she would have liked being bitten, she'd have laughed and called you crazy.

But this wasn't a pain-bite. It was Jacko's mouth knowing precisely how much pressure to bring to bear, the lightest possible bite, just enough to entice, not hurt. Once she'd climaxed through only a slight nip.

Jacko really knew his stuff.

But he once told her that it wasn't because he'd "fucked around" so much, as he put it. It was that he made a study of her. That he had touched or kissed every inch of skin on her and had memorized her reactions. He knew her body the way a concert pianist knows the keyboard, and he played it well.

She kissed him on the neck too. Because he knew her body but she also knew his. He made a low, rough sound, barely audible above the cascade of water. "I'm glad you're back," she whispered against his skin.

Jacko curled his big hand around her neck, lifting her chin with his thumb. Then his mouth was on hers again, the kiss deep and long. His hands traveled down her sides, reached her thighs and lifted.

His strength never ceased to amaze her. He lifted her as if she weighed nothing, hands under her thighs, spreading them apart, stepping forward between them. It was all just a feast for the senses. The waterfall of hot water, the heated scent of freesias, Jacko's hard body pinning her against the shower stall wall, his huge, hard penis probing to enter her.

"Damn," Jacko muttered against her mouth.

Lauren smiled and reached between them. "I thought you were this big-shot sniper. Infallible aim." She took his penis in hand and placed the head against her entrance. He was huge and burning hot.

"Little…distracted here," he mumbled against her mouth.

"Yeah?" Lauren licked his lips, opened her mouth against his and he groaned and leaned forward, pressing her more tightly to the wall. Jacko didn't plunge into her. She was always a little tight when he was gone for a few days and he was always careful. "Thought snipers never got distracted. Total focus. Ahh."

He slid into her, just the tip.

She wanted more. More, more, more.

Jacko had somehow changed her. She never used to be like this—sex-crazed. It was all his fault, turning her on so much. Giving her all these explosive orgasms. Then holding back now. Wasn't fair. The beast.

Lauren wriggled but there wasn't any purchase. With the wall at her back, and Jacko pressing so hard against her, she had no room to maneuver, nothing to force him to move.

Well...maybe something.

She clenched around him, hard, and felt him buck. "God, Lauren," he muttered. "Trying to be a gentleman."

"Mm. I don't want a gentleman, I want you." She closed her eyes, concentrated on her body. Everything in her felt full except her sex. It felt like her blood was going to escape her body, her skin was so tight; even her fingertips, pressed against Jacko's hard back, felt tight and tingling.

There was a remedy for that. Jacko had taught her. There was a remedy for that feeling of needing to explode.

"More," she whispered against his mouth and he pressed forward. Maybe halfway in. There was a lot of Jacko, and even half of him was more than most men. She had enough to work with now. Under the beating stream of hot water, she linked her ankles behind his back and writhed on him, almost dancing on him. There was just enough room for her to move up and down and circle him and oh God, it felt like she was burning up, that iron-hard rod unyielding and hot.

Jacko was saying something to her, something about the bed, but she wasn't listening. She couldn't. Every ounce of attention was centered on her body, between her legs, where Jacko barely penetrated her but was still the point of all pleasure in the world, gripping, blinding pleasure.

She circled him tightly, the moves echoing her mind, which was spiraling tightly around that pleasure spot, tighter and tighter...

With a wild cry, Lauren tipped over the edge, plunging into a deep abyss that would have scared her if she hadn't been held so tightly in Jacko's strong arms. The world fell away, disappeared and all that was left was her, Lauren, head tipped back against the wall, laughing. Happy her man was back.

Something penetrated her sleep. A sound, not enough to wake her. What woke her up was Jacko jackknifing up in bed and throwing back the covers. Cloth rustled as he pulled on jeans and a tee shirt.

It was dark in the room. She could barely see in the gloom, the only light coming from the full moon outside. Jacko had already finished dressing when she heard another sound, two notes this time. And she recognized the first sound she'd heard in her sleep.

The alarm.

The system Jacko had set up had two sound alarms. A single tone for when the outer perimeter of the property was breached and two tones for when someone was on the property. By some magical alchemy, Jacko had adjusted the setting so that no member of ASI or any of their women would set off the alarm. They joked about it—Metal could simply walk onto the property and throw a rock at their window and no alarm would be set off, not that Metal would ever do it.

Which was the point of the setting. Friends yes, foes no.

And for Jacko, if you weren't a friend, you were a foe.

A foe was at the door.

Lauren opened her mouth to say something to Jacko, who was checking his gun, the gun he kept within arm's reach. She'd learned enough about guns to see that he was freeing the magazine to check that it was loaded and sliding the chamber back to check that a bullet was already there.

Something was going to have to be done about that when their child started walking.

"Jacko, what—"

"Down," he said, voice low but not a whisper. "Keep down and don't go in the living room. Someone's on the property. Here…" He turned the monitor around so she could see it. The screen was split into four parts—front, back and both sides of the house. "So you can follow what's going on. But don't leave the room."

She nodded and he flowed out the door. There was no other word to describe it. He was there and suddenly he was not there. He was fast and quiet and smooth. She didn't hear his footsteps and she didn't hear the front door opening and closing.

There he was, on the panel that showed the front of the house, emerging then on the panel showing the side, meaning he'd stepped outside the front door.

Jacko's hands came up, fisted around his gun, and Lauren's heart started jackhammering. He edged forward sideways, making himself a smaller target, though Jacko was a huge target, even sideways. The view switched to the videocamera hidden in the bushes flanking the driveway. She could see his face in profile, expressionless, focused. He moved forward in small steps, which she knew kept his gun steady. Military steps, which meant he felt there was real danger.

He said something, though of course she couldn't hear what.

Then—then a look of utter astonishment crossed his face. She'd never seen that expression on him before, completely taken by surprise. She was trying to think what on earth could put that expression on Jacko's face—on the face of a man who'd seen just about everything—when she focused on a man next to Jacko's vehicle.

Jacko's eyes were wide and his gun hand dropped. Not in a controlled way, not because he'd received the order to put the gun down, but like someone who simply couldn't keep his hand up any longer.

Whatever it was out there was scaring Jacko. Or...not scaring him so much as astonishing him.

Should she go out there? If he lowered his gun, that meant—what did it mean? The man wasn't an enemy? What was going on? What did he see?

Jacko was simply standing there, doing nothing. Stock still. Eyes wide, jaw dropped.

And then *her* jaw dropped, because the man stood up slowly, hands open and to his sides, palms out. The universal sign of nonaggression, though his thumb held something against the palm of his right hand. Something small and square. He turned slightly so that he was fully captured by the security camera.

He looked—but no. That was impossible.

Lauren came closer to the camera, her breathing loud in the room. She put a hand to her mouth and stared at the monitor.

The man was large—as large as Jacko. He had close-cropped gray hair and was wearing a dark leather jacket. Except for his size, just a normal man. But he was anything but normal. What she saw had the hairs on her arms standing straight up.

His face. Dear God, his face.

He was the exact replica of Jacko. Except for the fact that he looked older, he could have been Jacko's twin. Identical twin.

CHAPTER NINE

Jacko felt like he'd been sucker punched. He could barely breathe. His lungs were trying to pull in air but the air had been sucked out of the night sky.

He'd caught the fucker red-handed. This big guy, hunkered down by the front right tire of Jacko's SUV. God knows what he was trying to do, because you don't boost a car from its chassis. But Jacko drew down on him. No matter what the fucker was trying to do, Jacko was calling the cops and the man would spend at least one night in jail. ASI knew everybody in the Portland PD, and he'd make sure the man got a good scare and wouldn't ever trespass again.

Then the man looked up and Jacko's gun hand went down.

He was nailed to the spot. Frozen. Couldn't move, couldn't think, couldn't breathe, couldn't talk.

It was like looking in a mirror.

The man standing not five feet from him was an exact copy of him. Face, height, size. Even the guy's hands looked like his. Shock reverberated through Jacko's system—the first time in his life he was shocked senseless.

The man stood at ease, hands out, holding something in the palm of his hand.

He searched Jacko's face with piercing eyes. The one thing that was different between them was that he had light gray eyes.

Who had talked about eyes lately?

Jacko couldn't reason through it, not with this mirror image standing right in front of him. Impossible, but very real. It wasn't a figment of his imagination and it wasn't a hologram. It was a flesh-and-blood man who looked exactly like him.

They stared at each other. Jacko could see a vein throbbing in the other man's neck. He felt a vein throbbing in his own neck.

Those light gray eyes shifted, watching his own. Jacko was mesmerized, was falling straight down into an abyss, his stomach swooping. He heard a whooshing sound inside his head.

The man spoke but the words didn't penetrate. Jacko could hardly hear him above the thunderous beating of his own heart.

"I didn't know about you until ten hours ago." Finally the words found a place in his head.

Jacko broke out of his frozen stance and shook his head. "What?"

"Can I move?"

Could he move? What the fuck kind of trick question was that? But then he realized he'd been rendered stupid by shock. What the guy was asking was would Jacko let him move without shooting him.

Because he still had a gun in his hand, finger inside the trigger guard. Anyone familiar with guns would recognize that as a signal that he was prepared to shoot.

Jacko removed his finger from the trigger guard. Which was crazy. He didn't know who the fuck this guy was who had invaded his property and was checking the undercarriage of his truck. But…he looked like Jacko. Surely his twin wouldn't attack him. Unless Jacko was batshit crazy and the only thing attacking him was his own head. "Yeah. You can move."

The man immediately stepped forward, inside Jacko's personal space, and put a hand on Jacko's shoulder. It was a sign of Jacko's stupefaction that he didn't knock that hand off. Nobody touched him that wasn't Lauren or a really good friend. But this hand felt…friendly.

Clearly Jacko was insane.

The man squeezed his shoulder. He had strong hands and it was a good thing Jacko had strong shoulders.

He stared straight into Jacko's eyes, light gray eyes set in a face just like his own. There was that whooshing sound in his head again.

"Son, you have to believe me when I say I had no idea you existed. When I got that call from Pendleton, it nearly buckled my knees." The man even sounded like Jacko. Voice deep, without Jacko's slight Texas twang.

"Pendleton?" Jacko's voice came out hoarse.

"Yeah, after you went to visit him in the home. I think the clouds in his head parted and he got in touch with me."

"Eyes," Jacko whispered, dazed. "He kept talking about my eyes. How they'd changed. He thought—he thought I was you."

"He did. He'd taken medication that morning that confused him. When it wore off, he realized he'd seen *you*. He'd kept your existence from me. He had his reasons and I'll explain them, but right now, I need to warn you that you're in trouble."

Jacko blinked. He felt slow, muscles mired in molasses, most of him numb. He was never this way in the battlefield. If he were, he'd be dead a thousand times over. But right now he was finding it hard to react while his mind was spinning.

"Trouble?" he repeated. It was hard enough believing what was right in front of his eyes, let alone that this man had brought trouble with him.

Trouble.

Lauren and their child were in the house.

Jacko lost that sense of shock and focused. "Who are you and why am I in trouble?" He pointed a thumb at the house. "My fiancée is in there. Tell me right now if she's in danger."

"I think you know who I am." The man waved at his face. "Who I am—what I am to you…is clear. All you have to do is look at us. My name is Dante Jimenez, I'm DEA, and thirty-five years ago I was stationed undercover in Cross, Texas."

"You met Sara Jackman," Jacko said tightly. "Met" meaning fucked.

Jimenez nodded sharply. "I did. It was a one-night stand. And I'm sorry to say I barely remember her and left soon after. But what you have to know now, Morton—"

"Jacko," he interrupted.

"Jacko." For the first time a faint smile crossed the man's features. "Better than Morton. What you have to know right now is that your vehicle was tracked."

"The fuck? My SUV has a company transponder. I turned it off."

"Not a transponder." Jimenez held his hand out, palm up. Jacko picked up the cheap plastic device with a magnet on one side. The ASI transponder was built into the vehicle. This was something else entirely.

"A tracking device."

"Yeah."

Jacko looked up and met those pale gray eyes. "Since when?"

"Since the sheriff's office in Cross. Guy's on the take, and he'll be taking from enemies of mine. What did you tell him?"

"Nothing. Not even my full name."

"Good. But he knows where you are now."

"Who? Who is this we're talking about? The sheriff?"

"No. Constable's a clown." Jimenez's face tightened. "I'm talking about a very dangerous man, son. And he'll be on his way with a team of shooters. So let's get inside and make plans."

They came in through the door and for just a second, Lauren had trouble distinguishing between the two. Then her brain unscrambled them. Jacko—shaved head, dark eyes. The other man—close-cropped, steel-wool gray hair, eerie gray eyes. But they looked that similar to each other.

First Jacko then the other man came in, bringing with them the chill night air and about a ton of testosterone.

Jacko walked over to her, put his arm around her waist and kissed her forehead. He turned her slightly. "Honey, this is Dante Jimenez. He's—"

"His dad. I'm Jacko's dad." Jimenez stuck out his big hand and Lauren stared at it. It was exactly like Jacko's hand—big and dark, same size, same shape. It was uncanny. She took the hand gingerly, felt him squeeze gently, then he let her hand go.

"I'm Lauren. Nice to meet you." The words came out automatically, the result of relentless maternal training in etiquette. But her head was whirling. *Was* it nice to meet him? What was he doing here? Why had Jimenez stayed away from Jacko all his life?

Jacko kept his big arm around her waist. He stared at...his father. How odd those words sounded in her head. "Lauren's pregnant. We're expecting a child." His face was hard, the words said harshly, as if Jimenez might somehow object.

The opposite happened. Jimenez's face melted. There was no other word for it. His face softened, eyes wide, jaw slightly dropped. "Oh God," he breathed. "A grandchild." He looked to one side for a moment, blinking, then turned back. "I never thought to have a son. And now a grandchild on the way. It's—it's almost too much." He narrowed his eyes. "We have to protect your family, son. The man who ordered the transponder? He will stop at nothing to hurt you, hurt Lauren, to get back at me."

Lauren froze, her hand going instinctively to her belly. "Who's going to hurt me?" she asked shakily.

Jacko's arm tightened. "No one. No one's going to hurt you, honey. Not while I'm alive."

"And not while I'm alive, either," Jimenez answered, and his expression was the exact same expression as Jacko's. Tight and grim. He switched his gaze to Jacko. "The enemy is Carlos Villalongo, son of the head of the Laredo cartel. I'm DEA and I put his father away. He died in prison. I've been after the cartel my entire career, and he just found out that you're my son. We intercepted a conversation. He wants to use you as leverage to get to me, but that's not going to happen. We need to secure Lauren and then we need to arm up and strategize. I have some men coming."

"Who?" Jacko sounded suspicious. "And how am I supposed to tell the bad guys from the good guys?"

"The good guys will be wearing DEA blazers. And they'll be here in—" He held a finger up as a cell phone buzzed. "Yeah, Jimenez. Give me some good news." He listened, eyes narrowed. "Fuck. You tracking Villalongo? When?"

Jacko dropped his arm around her waist and stepped up to Jimenez. He grabbed a fistful of jacket and got right into his face. "Goddammit, you tell me right now what's going on, who's threatening Lauren, or I swear to God I'll hurt you."

Jimenez made no attempt to defend himself. "I hear you. The thing is, we don't have much time. My men are stuck in a snowstorm and are contacting local DEA agents, but they will have to bring them up to speed. The first thing I need to know, is there somewhere we can put Lauren where she'll be safe and can you call in any members of your security team? I googled your company on the way over and it looks like you've got some good men there. Can you call on them?"

Jacko released Jimenez's jacket and dug out his cell. He spoke, keeping his eyes on Jimenez. "Yo. Code red here. You and Joe back yet, because I've got a…DEA agent who says a cartel boss named Villalongo is coming here. Can you get Felicity to do some research?" So he was talking to Metal. "I need Lauren secured and I need boots on the ground here because the agent's guys are stuck in a snowstorm. Come geared up. Yeah." He cocked his head at Jimenez. "How much time we got?"

Jimenez's mouth tightened. "They might have already landed at Portland International."

"Fuck. Hear that? Yeah, come fast and get Lauren out of here." He looked at Lauren. "My guys are still out of town, heading in. He says another thirty minutes at least. Maybe you should pack something, honey. Just in case."

Her heart thudded in her chest. *Pack?* Was he expecting a siege? Was he expecting not to live through it? "Why pack? Oh God, Jacko, what's happening? What's coming for us?"

He folded her in his arms and she clung to him, to his massively strong body, breathing in his familiar scent. Their bodies clicked together like magnets and she knew exactly where to nestle against him

"You seem to have a good crew here," Jimenez said to Jacko.

"The best," Jacko answered over her head. Her cheek was against his chest and the familiar rumble of his voice calmed her. "And we have the best IT person in the world. She's going to find out everything about Villalongo, down to the size of his briefs."

Jimenez shook his head. "Should have had her with me these past years. He went underground, had a hell of a time tracking him, the fucker. Pardon me, ma'am."

Lauren gave a shaky smile against Jacko's chest. "If I understand things correctly, there are killers coming. There might be a shootout. Someone could die. I can take some crude language."

"Jacko," Jimenez said. "You got gear? I was only able to bring my service piece, four mags and this." He thumped himself on the chest and a hollow sound erupted. "Body armor."

Jacko nodded tightly. "I got gear."

That was like Brangelina saying they had kids. Jacko had *gear*.

He pulled away and held her by the shoulders, away from him. "It's okay. Metal's coming. He'll be here soon. You'll be safe."

Lauren hooked her hands on his strong forearms. "And you?" She hated that her voice quavered. But there wasn't anything she could do. Deep in her heart, she'd always feared that Jacko had used up his nine lives as a Navy SEAL. That he was living on borrowed time. "I can't lose you, Jacko. *We* can't lose you."

His eyes widened. He did that every single time she worried about him, as if it were impossible for someone to be worried about *him*.

"Don't worry about me, honey. As long as I know you're safe, I'll be fine." He shook his head a little, kissed her on the forehead and moved away.

He walked over to Jimenez—to the man who was his father. The two men stood quietly conferring, heads tilted toward each other. For a second it was like an optical illusion—like a man in a mirror instead of two men. Jacko led his father to what had once been a large hallway closet and was now a war room, bristling with weaponry. Some men had come one morning, lined the panels with metal, put in a fancy keypad next to the door, lined the door with something that looked like it should be shot into space, and then made the outer part of the door look like an ordinary wooden closet door. The keypad was disguised too. No one could tell from the outside that inside was enough weaponry to wage war on a small country.

Jacko disengaged the lock on the keypad, which slid open. He entered the code and then his thumbprint and the door unlocked with a snick. Jacko casually pushed the bank-vault quality door open, though Lauren knew for a fact that it weighed a ton. She'd barely been able to move it an inch.

The two men disappeared inside. She shifted so she could see what they were doing.

They were putting together an arsenal in record time, communicating in some kind of code made up of single words.

It was amazing. The two men had met only a few minutes ago and yet they were working together as if they'd been partners for years. She'd once watched Jacko, Metal and Joe gear up for what they called red team/blue team exercises, and the three men had worked like that. Quietly, efficiently and fast, according to some pre-set system of rules only they understood.

Inside of five minutes, Jacko and Jimenez were standing outside in the corridor with weapons stacked neatly beside them.

"Here. Arms up." Lauren's arms went up as Jacko fit a bulletproof vest over her head, pulling the tapes tight. He'd insisted on having one custom-made for her. He said he couldn't stand the thought of having several of his own while she had none. She'd tried on one of his and it was like wearing a very heavy barrel. She couldn't move with the damned thing on.

As he pressed the tapes together, she looked down at herself, the gray silk nightgown flowing out from the bottom edge. She touched her chest, ran her hand along the front of the vest. In about eight months, the vest wouldn't fit over her belly. Did the manufacturers make pregnant-lady vests?

Probably not.

Jacko and Jimenez worked so well together, so seamlessly, that it was easy to miss the speed. Very little time had passed and they were ready to go to war.

It was terrifying. A deep shudder ripped through her, seeing the men moving so quietly and efficiently, readying to do battle. She'd never seen Jacko like this before. He was usually a serious man, though not quite as grim as when she'd first met him. But now it was like he was imbued with some special warrior mojo. He and Jimenez both looked strong, implacable, invincible.

But they weren't. No one was invincible. Bullets respected no man. The people who were coming must be serious bad guys to evoke this kind of response.

Thank God she hadn't known Jacko in his SEAL years, where every day he faced the worst kind of enemy.

Another shudder ran through her and she had to stiffen her knees to remain upright. Jacko noticed and reached to get her coat. He dropped it around her shoulders, mistaking her fear for him for cold. She wasn't cold, she was scared.

"Don't have time to get you dressed, honey," he said. "Put on your boots, though." He knelt and slipped on her soft suede boots, without socks. He was moving so fast! In a second he was up and reaching for his gun, a huge black thing that looked like you could kill aliens with it.

A two-note tone sounded, soft, echoing in the silence.

Another spasm of fear gripped her.

Jacko looked at Jimenez. "They're here." He turned to her, opening the gun vault door wide. "In you go, honey."

Lauren froze, looking into the blackness of the vault. She was mildly claustrophobic. The idea of stepping inside and being locked in...she shuddered. Panic gripped her insides.

Jacko put a gentle hand to her back and moved her forward, past the threshold. She had to force her feet to move. She didn't want to go into that blackness, closed up like in a tomb but she understood Jacko. He needed to know she was safe. Being inside the vault made her feel like she was buried alive but she was definitely safe from flying bullets.

She turned to look at him, biting her lips to keep from crying. A spasm shook her body but she gave no sign. She looked at his face, wondering if it was the last time she'd see him alive.

Jacko's face was hard, set. He reached to the side to switch on a light so she wouldn't be stuck in the dark. "The code to open the door is 17629 and the keypad is to the right. Don't open to anyone but me. If I don't come for you, Metal knows the code and will open the door."

Meaning—*if I'm killed you won't be buried alive here.*

He swung the vault door shut and it locked with a sinister snick. She was trapped in here and Jacko was facing men with guns.

Her belly cramped with a fierce pain that made her stumble. She looked down. Jacko had had the vault lined with white tiles, easy to keep clean. She blinked and felt her stomach lurch when she saw red drops.

Blood.

She looked down at herself. Past the lower edge of the vest, the light gray of her nightgown showed patches of black. Another cramp and the black patch grew.

She curled in on herself, hand pressed to her belly, holding on, as if pressing against herself could stop the terrible thing that was happening.

She was losing the baby.

CHAPTER TEN

His father was an operator, not a wasted movement.

Jimenez glanced at him, and knew he didn't have to voice the question that was burning inside him. *She okay?*

Jacko nodded, as if he'd heard the words. "She'll be safe."

They both studied the array of monitors. The top right-hand one was IR and showed four figures on the perimeter—two in front, two in back. The IR was very spotty.

"Ballistic materials," Jimenez said, and Jacko nodded. Some form of Nomex or Teflon-based tactical gear that masked body heat. "Villalongo's guys aren't this good. He's gone all out and hired outside muscle. He wants you bad."

"Well, he can't have me." Jacko's cell pinged. Felicity. He put it on speakerphone, volume low. "Talk to me," he said.

"You've got four operators," she said, "But you'll see that already. They all drove in a big van that's parked on Oakland, facing east. There's one operator still in the vehicle. Metal and Joe are coming as fast as they can. They'll approach from the rear. Do me a favor and don't shoot Metal by mistake. Tell your…guy."

It had been so weird telling Felicity that the man he was with was his father. Evidently she was finding it weird, too.

"Jacko." Jimenez grabbed his arm, held tight. They were exactly the same height and Jimenez stared him in the eyes, face right up next to his. "The guy in the vehicle is Carlos, I'll bet you anything. His father would have gone in with the operators, but Carlos was always a wuss, waiting for others to do his dirty work. But make no mistake." Jimenez's pale eyes narrowed. "He'll keep coming after me and he won't hesitate to hurt Lauren and the baby. He needs to be taken out now, for good. No matter what. You read me?"

Jacko did.

"Let me do it," Jimenez continued. "I don't want any blowback coming back on you. I need to end this."

On the screens, two men brought up thermal binoculars.

"They won't see Lauren but they'll see us," Jimenez said.

"No. I had Lauren's house painted with a refractive paint. They can't see in to count how many we are. And the windows are coated too. The house is dead to them. We'll wait inside, let them break their way in."

"Good tactical advantage. They know your background?"

Meaning: Did they know Jacko was a Navy SEAL?

"I don't think so. I think all they have to go on is that my vehicle stopped in this driveway. I just gave Constable my last name. And my vehicle is registered to a special entity my company set up for this purpose. So no one can trace any of the company vehicles back to us specifically. No, I think they're moving in blind."

Jimenez nodded sharply. "That's good. We're going to take these fuckers *down.*" He met Jacko's eyes, his own pale eyes blazing. "Gustavo Villalongo ordered a woman I loved killed in 2004. That's not going to happen again to anyone I care about. The Villalongos are over. Nothing is going to happen here, no more losses. And no mercy."

No. They were coming and Lauren was in the crossfire. No mercy. Shit no.

Jacko handed Jimenez a comms unit and fitted his own to his ear. He tapped and heard Felicity. "Okay, we're all online, comms secure. Metal's almost— *Jacko!*" Felicity's usually calm voice turned frantic. "Intruders going weapons hot, I repeat—"

Jimenez pushed Jacko to the ground as a huge hole opened up in the wall next to the front door. Then another and another.

Deafening noise, almost as bad as a flashbang, splinters flying everywhere. It had to be a Mossberg or similarly powerful shotgun. The rounds went through the walls and shattered whatever they found in their way. The couch exploded and a cupboard full of china shattered in a million shards.

"Goddamn," Jacko growled. "That stuff has been in Lauren's family for 150 years."

"She's gonna be pissed," Jimenez warned.

"Big time," Jacko agreed. The two men looked at each other, and then, crazily, Jimenez grinned. Jacko could feel the grin on his own face.

"Fuckers fucked with the wrong guys," he said.

"Damn straight, they fucked with the wrong guys," Jimenez agreed. "We go to the windows. On three." He held up a hand that looked exactly like Jacko's hand, three fingers up. Two. One.

Go!

They each rushed to a window. Jimenez would be familiar with the special coating Jacko had put on all the windows. It completely blocked everything from the outside in. Not even thermal imaging would show anything to anyone outside the house. But it allowed light—full-spectrum light—in. He and Jimenez could see out but the attackers couldn't see in.

Two men were rushing the house. Jacko and Jimenez shouldered their rifles and shot at the exact same second, two men dropping like sacks of meat.

The crackle of automatic fire sounded in the back and they both rushed down the corridor to the back wall.

The windows were gone and so was their cover. Jimenez crouched with his back to the wall under the window, counted down, stood, turned, aimed out the window and shot, then dropped back down. A scream sounded outside in the back yard.

Three down, one left. Bullets sprayed the back of the house. Fuck!

Jacko was scared. Scared shitless. It was a new sensation for him. In battle there was a part of his mind that switched off, and it was the part that controlled emotions. He felt nothing in battle. His entire being was pure mathematical calculation. He could count bullets, he moved his body precisely through space, he knew where he was in relation to other markers and other shooters.

Not now. Now he was a hot mess of emotions, and on top of the steamy mess of shit was fear. Until the danger was neutralized, Lauren was at risk. There were all sorts of scenarios where she didn't come out of this unharmed. She was in the vault, but if they killed him and Jimenez and torched the place, she'd be burned alive. The image of a hurt or dying Lauren flooded his head.

He felt awkward, clumsy, slow. The gun in his hand felt heavy and awkward, though he'd clocked thousands of hours on it at the range.

But he had muscle memory, and that was what had him bringing up his Glock at the hint of a shadow on the wall and his mind worked out trajectory and distance all on its own when he saw the shadow and calculated the height as he was pulling the trigger, a perfect double tap to the head and the guy's brains were painted on the wall.

He tapped his ear. "Last one down."

He heard Jimenez in his ear. "You go see to your lady. I've got business to attend to."

All clear.

He rushed to the gun vault, keyed in the code, pulled the heavy door open.

She was crouched on the ground, skin paper white, eyes huge, beautiful face pinched. She drew in a breath when she saw him.

"It's okay, honey," he said reflexively, bending down to help her up, then froze.

It wasn't okay.

She'd been shot. How on earth could she have been wounded in here? But there was no mistaking it. Blood was seeping out from under the lower edge of her body armor. He couldn't tell where she'd been shot.

"My God!" Jacko opened his hands but didn't pull her up. He was terrified of touching her until he knew where the bullet wound was. He could hurt her badly.

Jacko dropped to his knees next to her, taking her hand. At least he could touch her there.

"Where were you shot, baby?" He barely recognized his own voice. It was hoarse, guttural, pure desperation in the form of sound.

He tapped his earbud. "Metal! Where are you?" Metal always carried medical essentials in his SUV, including a gurney with a neck brace. "Lauren's been shot!"

"Almost there," Metal's calm voice came in. "Where are you?"

"Gun vault!" He nearly screamed the words.

Jacko turned to Lauren. "Where've you been shot, honey? Metal's coming. You're going to be fine. We'll get you to the hospital as soon as possible."

Her mouth opened, closed. Her jaws clenched as a wave of pain went through her and Jacko nearly died. "Honey? Where are you wounded?"

"Not. Shot." She gasped, clenching her teeth.

But… "You *are* shot, honey. You're bleeding!"

"Not. Gunshot. Wound." She could talk only one word at a time. One bloody hand held on to him, the other was curled protectively around her belly. "It's the baby."

Jacko felt stupid with terror. He couldn't follow her. "What?"

She gulped in air and spoke fast, eyes huge and fixed on his face. "The baby, Jacko. I'm losing the baby."

This ends here and now, Jimenez thought grimly. His son's IT person had shown him a map of the block over his cell and Jimenez had memorized it. He read maps well and he made his way unerringly through back yards, only hoping he wouldn't cross a dog. A meticulously planned DEA drug raid had once been derailed by a guard dog in a neighboring yard.

But fate intervened and he encountered no dogs. Damn straight. Fate, that bitch, had deprived him of a son for over thirty years and the least she could do was ride alongside him tonight while he put an end to this.

His son.

While Jimenez made his way swiftly and quietly to the street where he was sure Carlos waited, automatically seeking cover against trees and bushes, his head whirled. A son. *His* son.

God.

Jimenez was nearing the end of his career in the DEA. He knew he was a legend. He'd done some good, but once he retired, that would be it for him. He'd dedicated his life to the DEA. He'd never married and had only loved one woman. Deanna.

They'd had to keep their love a secret because Villalongo had a big reward on his head. Someone ratted him out and Villalongo's thugs had killed Deanna. She'd died in his arms. After which, Jimenez had unleashed hell on earth on the cartel, decimating the ranks.

The Villalongo cartel was almost finished, thanks to him. He thought that would be his legacy.

Instead, he had a son. All those long, lonely years fighting a once-strong cartel, he'd had a son. And what a son. Jacko's jacket was closed to the public but he could access it, and had on the flight from Washington to Portland. His son was an incredible sniper and had medals for bravery coming out of his ass.

Jiminez also had an idea of what Jacko's childhood must have been like. Hell on earth. Sara was already a good-time girl when he met her while undercover in Cross. She thought he was in the cartel. She'd *liked* the idea that he was a drug dealer. It got her off. They'd had a one-night stand and Jimenez hadn't given her another thought, but he'd left a child behind in the care of a junkie.

He'd been DEA all his life. He knew what junkies were like.

Jacko'd risen above that, made a real success of his life. Jimenez had felt an instant bond with the man—and God, his woman was pregnant. A grandchild. A fucking grandchild. This time he wouldn't mess it up. This time he'd be there for the kid the way he hadn't been for Jacko.

He had his back to a fence, weapon up, looking at his cell. Jacko's IT person, called Felicity, had sent him the infrared image of the street. Either she was hooked up to satellites—which was impressive—or had sent drones—which was even more impressive.

Four vehicles on the street, three empty, engines cold.

One right around the corner, a van, with a man at the wheel, the engine pale yellow. Once warm, now cooling.

The back of the van was empty. They were planning on either kidnapping or killing Jacko.

He smiled grimly to himself. *Good luck with that, you fucker*, he thought. Carlos had no idea who or what Jacko was. All Carlos knew was that hurting him would hurt Jimenez.

You're done hurting me and mine.

Jimenez rounded the corner fast, weapon up.

Be armed, be armed, he chanted to himself as he made his way quietly to the driver's side of the vehicle. If Carlos was armed, he could end this quickly. A shot to the head, and it was self-defense. No one was going to look too closely. Everyone knew that Carlos had made Dante's life hell for decades. And it was always good to have one more scumbag in the ground.

The idiot was looking at something—a small screen. The glow lit his face from below, making him look like the monster he was.

Draw on me, motherfucker, he thought as he tapped on the window.

The temptation to just shoot him right now was so strong sweat formed on Dante's forehead. This man and his father had ruined his life, had been the cause of endless suffering, had wrecked the lives of two generations of kids. The father was dead and this man had no right to be among the living.

Just shoot him. Get it over with.

But Dante had taken an oath and believed in the justice system. Sort of. Of course Villalongo would lawyer up, just like his dad had done, and would spend a long time out of prison waiting for trial, but right now he'd made an attempt on the life of a federal agent and a former Navy SEAL and a young woman. He wasn't going to get out of this.

Dante didn't want him hauled before a court, subjected to a long, drawn-out trial then put in jail. Dante wanted him dead.

Villalongo looked up, startled out of his contemplation of the screen. Thinking he was watching the takedown of someone important to Dante.

No, sir, Dante thought. Not this time.

Please try to kill me. He sent up that little prayer. He'd never asked for anything before. Give him this. Let Villalongo make an attempt on his life and spare the state the expense of a trial and free Dante from a decades-old fight. Let Villalongo be stupid just one last time. Please.

And...yes!

Villalongo's eyes widened, his hand reached for the Sig Sauer on the passenger seat, he brought it around two-handed, started pressing the trigger...

And Dante shot him in the forehead, splattering his brains all over the inside of the van.

He lowered his weapon slowly, peering through the shattered glass at a dead Carlos Villalongo.

He felt nothing. Not sadness and not joy.

All he felt was a burning desire to get back to his son, his son's pretty lady and their child. His grandchild.

In the death and misery of the Villalongo saga, there was also new life and a new beginning.

He ran back to the house, in through the front door and stopped, almost skidding. The house was still dark. He would have expected Jacko and his lady to be picking up the pieces, maybe find her crying over the shattered china. But there was silence.

Dante flipped on the lights and at the same time, he heard a cry. A woman's cry. Was Jacko wounded? God...dead?

His heart pounding in his chest, he shot to the gun vault. The door was open and he could see a living Jacko bending over a living Lauren and he stopped, relieved.

Until he saw the blood.

Dante swallowed. "She shot?"

Jacko was kneeling next to her, Lauren clinging to him. There was blood on her nightgown under the vest.

"You can take that vest off, if she's uncomfortable."

Jacko shot him a sharp look. "You sure?"

"Yeah. I just killed Carlos. It's over." He took a step toward them. "Where's she shot, how can I help?"

Jacko was moving fast toward the front door with Lauren in his arms. He dug in a ceramic bowl near the front door, tossed a set of keys to Dante. Dante caught the set one-handed.

"We're going to the hospital. You're driving, I'll navigate. Let's go."

Dante followed him out, pressing the fob that opened the doors to Jacko's SUV. While Jacko got in the back with Lauren, carefully setting her on the seat, Dante got behind the wheel. He checked the rearview mirror and as soon as Jacko settled Lauren in and closed the door, he took off fast.

"At the third intersection, turn left. Then it's a straight ride to the hospital, go around to the A & E side."

"Got it." Dante met Lauren's eyes in the mirror. "I'm so sorry you got shot, honey," he said gently. "We'll get you patched up."

"Not shot," Jacko said grimly. "She's losing the baby."

Dante's heart gave a huge thump in his chest and he floored the accelerator. "No," he said. "I won't let her lose that baby. That's my grandchild."

EPILOGUE

Eight months later

Lauren stopped in her slow shuffle down the hospital corridor, holding on to Jacko's shoulder. So far she'd been amazingly brave. And calm.

Jacko himself was jumping out of his skin. He'd done a lot of reading about childbirth, though most of what he read terrified him. So many fucking things could go so terribly wrong. It was amazing, the list of things that could go wrong. As a matter of fact, it seemed like a miracle to him that most people managed to get born just fine.

The night Dante came into their lives, Lauren had almost lost the baby. He still got the shivers when he thought of those couple of hours while the doctors fought for their baby, and in the end won.

They told him that Lauren had to take it easy. Oh yeah. He made sure of that, to the point she complained that she wasn't allowed to do anything.

Well, maybe he'd been a bit heavy-handed, but here she was, giving birth.

"They're coming five minutes apart," Lauren gasped and Jacko wanted to kick himself in the ass. That was his job—to time the contractions. She was getting ready to push a human being through a small orifice and his only job was to glance at his watch when she had a contraction. How hard could that be for a SEAL?

Hard, apparently, because he kept forgetting.

Contractions every five minutes. That was good, right? Or not. The fuck he knew. Every single thing he'd read about childbirth had completely flown from his mind.

Lauren glanced up at his face and smiled at him and patted his shoulder.

Jesus, she was calming *him* down!

She started up again, that slow shuffle. They'd been going up and down the corridor for hours, it felt like.

"So," she said. "Where's Grandpa?"

"Outside," Jacko answered. "He said he needed some fresh air."

She huffed out a breath and shook her head. "Needed a cigar, more like it," she said.

"Yeah, that too. But he said he'd be back soon."

"They won't let him in the delivery room."

"No, he knows that. He'll be outside waiting with everyone else."

They were all there, outside. Waiting. ASI had a skeleton staff as everyone who could be spared was here, waiting for the baby to be born.

"She's going to have a big family, but I'm really glad she's going to have a grandfather."

"Yeah," Jacko said hoarsely. He cleared his voice. Dante was going to make a fantastic grandfather. He'd retired from the DEA and moved to Portland, where he became everyone's favorite geezer. Well, not a geezer, not really. Guy still had juice in him. He'd done a couple of contract jobs for ASI where an investigator was needed, and had excelled. Midnight and the Senior had offered him full-time employment but he'd refused. He wanted to be a full-time grandpa. He said he'd missed out on Jacko and wanted to make up for it with his granddaughter.

Dante Jimenez was a permanent part of their lives. Jacko still found it hard to think of him as a father, but it was easy to think of him as a really, really good friend who just happened to look exactly like him.

Lauren stopped and hunched over, eyes closed.

"Four minutes," she said. "I think we should be going back. I think we're getting close."

Getting close. Oh God. All of a sudden he wanted to stop the clock, tell Lauren...what? Stop labor? He wasn't ready for this, he wasn't sure at all that he was going to be a good daddy. He told Lauren that once, and she'd just laughed. Said he was born to be a dad.

Where did she get *that* from? How could she tell?

Jacko kept pace with Lauren and she walked slowly, slowly down the corridor to the delivery room. He would have given anything to just pick her up and carry her there, but she didn't want that. She wanted to get there by herself.

Finally, after about eight billion years and several stops while she had contractions, they got to the delivery room.

Lauren stopped on the threshold, looked at the nurse and whispered, "A minute apart."

Two nurses came over and, in their brisk, efficient manner, took Lauren from him, put her on a cot with those awful stirrup things and fit her feet to the stirrups.

He heard Lauren moan and if he didn't have a shaved head, every hair on his head would have stood up.

Then things got a little hazy. There was pain and there was blood and it all drove him a little crazy. Through it all, Lauren was incredibly brave and calm, holding on to his hand so hard it almost hurt.

He'd *trained* for this. A thousand lessons with other pregnant women and their partners, practicing timed breathing and backrubs. He completely forgot everything he'd learned, forgot how to coach her breathing and couldn't do anything but cling to her hand and sweat.

Then things got really bad, and there was a *lot* of blood. He'd been in the field, he'd been shot himself, but this was much, much worse. The nurses grew very quiet, working efficiently, doing things he didn't understand, and then the doctor came and sat on a stool between Lauren's raised legs and spoke in a low, calm voice, and then there was even more blood...

Jacko's knees grew weak.

No one bothered to tell him what the fuck was going on. They spoke in quiet monosyllables, words that made no sense to him. Jacko was at the head of the bed and couldn't see what was going on but nearly freaked when the doctor took a fucking scalpel and made an incision.

Jacko was about ready to attack the doctor when there was a flurry of movement at the foot of the bed and—

A cry. A baby's cry. Lauren, who was covered in sweat, gave a weak laugh.

"What's her Apgar score?" she asked in an exhausted voice.

The doctor pulled down his mask and smiled. "A hundred," he said, and Lauren laughed again. That was one thing Jacko knew. The Apgar score was the indicator of the health of a newborn baby, a score that went from one to ten. Ten being perfect.

Suddenly one of the nurses thrust a blanket-covered thing in his arms. Startled, Jacko let go of Lauren and looked down.

She was small and warm. Tiny, perfect features. A fuzz of dark hair, smooth, soft olive skin.

She opened her eyes and he nearly gasped. They were silver-blue and they were looking right at him. All the books said babies couldn't focus. They started seeing things at four months, but Jacko knew that little Alice, named for the grandmother she'd never know, was looking at *him*.

And then she smiled. To his dying day, he'd swear she smiled at him in the first minutes of her life.

Jacko's heart moved from his chest to hers and for the second time in his life, he fell in love.

The End

Dear reader, I hope you enjoyed this book. If you did, I'd appreciate a review on the Amazon page and/or on Goodreads. If you liked this book, you might also enjoy:

THE MIDNIGHT TRILOGY
1. Midnight Man
2. Midnight Run
3. Midnight Angel

The Midnight Trilogy Box Set

THE MEN OF MIDNIGHT
1. Midnight Vengeance
2. Midnight Promises
3. Midnight Secrets
4. Midnight Fire

MIDNIGHT NOVELLA
Midnight Shadows

Woman on the Run
Murphy's Law

THE DANGEROUS TRILOGY
Dangerous Lover
Dangerous Secrets
Dangerous Passion

THE PROTECTORS TRILOGY
Into the Crossfire
Hotter than Wildfire
Nightfire

GHOST OPS TRILOGY
Heart of Danger
I Dream of Danger
Breaking Danger

NOVELLAS
Fatal Heat
Hot Secrets
Reckless Night

ACKNOWLEDGMENTS

Thanks to my great agent, Christine Witthohn, and wonderful editor, Kelli Collins. And a special thanks to my assistant, Kim Golden, who does all the hard stuff.

ABOUT THE AUTHOR

Lisa Marie Rice is eternally 30 years old and will never age. She is tall and willowy and beautiful. Men drop at her feet like ripe pears. She has won every major book prize in the world. She is a black belt with advanced degrees in archaeology, nuclear physics, and Tibetan literature. She is a concert pianist. Did I mention her Nobel Prize? Of course, Lisa Marie Rice is a virtual woman and exists only at the keyboard when writing romance. She disappears when the monitor winks off.